The Unexpected Reunion

L. Clara

First Edition published by 2024

Copyright © 2024 by L. Clara

Edited by Nikki Grant

Cover Design by Nerd Sisters Designs

If you are reading this content anywhere other than Amazon or Kindle/Kindle Unlimited you are reading a pirated copy. Please reach out to me directly with the link at <u>lcturnspages@gmail.com</u>

For the girls, gays, and theys who have been told to dim your light. Shine as bright as you can, babe. This one is for you.

Contents

Trigger Warnings

Homophobia

Parental neglect/rejection,

Mention of Domestic Violence

Suicide attempt (on page)

Bullying

Sexually explicit scenes

This is a duet so please note that there will be a cliffhanger.

Note from the author

If you or anyone you know is struggling with their sexuality or need general support please call the General LGBT Hotline at 888-843-4564.

For additional LGBTQIA support lines please visit https://lgbthotline.org/

If you or anyone you know is a victim of domestic violence, please reach out for help.

National Domestic Violence Hotline 1-800-799-7233 Text "START" to 88788

If you or anyone you know is struggling with suicidal thoughts or going through a crisis, you can call or text the 988 Lifeline, which provides 24/7, free, and confidential support. Call or text them by dialing 988 or live message/chat with them at their website: https://988lifeline.org

C*ollege*

Sunlight shines through open slats of the blinds from the window next to where I sit on my twin size bed in the dorm suite I share with my assigned roommate, Becca. She's never home, constantly staying at her boyfriend's apartment or out with friends. So, I guess I can't complain. The suite is spacious, giving us each our own bedroom, and then a shared kitchen and living room area.

I look up at the woman standing before me. She's gorgeous as always, the natural light gives her an angelic glow. She's wearing a pair of the smallest shorts I've ever seen, which show off her tan and impressively toned legs. I want her, God, I've wanted her since the first day we met. She's beautiful, funny, sassy, she's everything I want in a partner. She's staring down at me; her long golden locks are pulled back in French braid pigtails showing off her high cheekbones that most women would kill for. Her beautiful round eyes that resemble the ocean are on full display. Only her eyes look sad today.

"What's going on, Bunny?" My nickname for her slips out so easily. My hand darts out for hers, my constant need to comfort her apparent as always. Only after my skin touches hers does she find her words.

"I, I can't do this anymore, Pickle." Anya chokes out the silly nickname she gave me when she saw me with an entire lunch bag of assorted pickles to snack on during an afternoon class.

"What do you mean, this?" I ask as I tighten my hand around her wrist, I stand up to meet her gaze.

"They're going to disown me; I can't lose my family." The tears flow freely as she collapses against me.

I drop her wrist and wrap my arms around her tiny frame. Holding onto her as she lets the sobs wreck through her. Lost in my memories of when my own parents disowned me. The only family I can honestly claim anymore are my siblings, Augustus or Auggie but he won't let anyone but me call him that, and Penny well, kind of. It could be seconds, minutes or hours before I register, I haven't responded. I'm really not sure. When my brain functions again, I softly press against Anya's shoulders to look at her. Delicately gripping her jaw, I tip her chin up to look at me through her tear-filled eyes.

"I love you, Bunny. I'm not sure what else I can say here. You know I love you." I take a deep breath. "You need to decide what you want. Do you want to live for your family or for yourself?"

"Pickle, I, I don't know." She's beginning to hyperventilate.

I stand from my bed, helping her sit down and run out to the kitchen to grab a brown paper bag from on top of the fridge. When I return, I open the bag and seal the opening to her mouth to help her catch her breath. It takes a few moments before she calms down. "Let me get you home, okay?"

With a gentle nod in agreement, I help her stand and throw on a hoodie before we head into the cool summer night air. The walk to her building is quiet, neither of us having much to say to each other after her declaration back in my room. My heart is hoping that I wake up tomorrow and this will all be some twisted nightmare, but I know that won't be the case. Finally reaching her dorm, I lead her up the stairs to the third floor and take Anya to her room. When I get her settled in her room, I press a soft kiss to her forehead. "I love you, Bunny. When you make your decision, you know where to find me, yeah?"

I climb the stairs to my floor, stopping at the landing before pulling open the door to the hall my dorm is on. Leaning flush against the wall, I slide down to the floor, my face buried in my hands. The tears that have been fighting their way to the surface since she came to me this afternoon have finally broken through. Silently, I allow my emotions to flow before I have to face my siblings who have been cautious of Anya since our relationship began, because every time we got close, she would push me away. It's never been to this extreme, though.

Once the anguish subsides enough for me to climb back to my feet, I take the walk of shame back to my door. As soon as I turn the knob and push the door open, Becca is there with a bottle of whiskey in one hand and a jar of pickle juice in the other.

"I've kind of been home and heard." She frowns at me, her dark hair is wet like she just got out of the shower. "I know we're not the best of friends, but I don't want you to be alone. I don't really do words for something like this," she pauses briefly as she pours the amber liquid into a shot glass. "Let's drink."

I don't bother to respond with words, I just take the bottle of whiskey and chug before taking the pickle juice and doing the same.

"I'm afraid I'm never going to see her again." I cough as the mixture of whiskey and pickle juice collide in the depths of my throat.

She brings a bottle of Corona up to her lips, taking a long sip. "I'm just here to be your emotional support drunk tonight. Cheers." She lifts her bottle for me to clink.

I've polished off the bottle of whiskey, and Becca has finished a six-pack. I'm mid crawl into the bathroom to puke my guts out when I feel something hard and warm caging me in and lifting me from underneath my arms.

"Come on, kid. On your feet, I've got you." I hear a soothing, gravelly voice as my eyes flutter open when I feel myself floating into the air onto my feet.

"Hi, Auggie. You were right. She left me." It comes out as a cross between a giggle and a sob.

"I don't know who Auggie is. Let's just get you taken care of, and we can talk about it when the inevitable hangover subsides." The warm cage doesn't put me down until we're in the bathroom and he moves to hold my hair back off my neck when the unknown number of picklebacks make their way back up my digestive tract.

I wake up to the feel of a cool surface below me. Opening my eyes, I realize I'm back in the bathroom, or did I never leave? Stretching my limbs, I feel stiff as hell like I slept on the floor. Crap. I climb to my feet and immediately regret my life choices when everything that was left in my stomach decides to make its way back up and out the hatch.

Oh, Linda Blair would be so proud.

"Ugggggghhhh," I groan into the empty space.

Before I've had any time to process what's happening, the bathroom door swings open just as a familiar voice fills the space. I've never seen him before but the bright smile on his face has me weak in the knees. He's got a glass of water in one hand and a few Advil in the other.

"Good morning, beautiful."

I should be terrified of this stranger being in my home. The only thing I feel in his presence is safety.

"I don't know you, but I hate you." I cringe at the peppiness.

"That's unfortunate, but let's see if we can change that. I'm Clay." He passes me the pills and liquid. "Becca asked me to hang out until you came to. I moved in down the hall a few weeks ago. She asked me to help get you in here last night because she was worried about how much you drank."

"Listen, let the pain killers kill the pain, then we can discuss my feelings on you and your joyful existence." I gag as I lift to my knees and dry-heave over the commode. "Go away."

He doesn't respond, at least not with words. He stands beside me, holding my long dark hair out of my face and off my neck again.

Chapter One

Six years later

The sounds of free-weights clanking as I step into my safe space is like music to my ears. I look around Karma, a large open room with equipment ranging from treadmills and ellipticals to weight machines and free-weights. Toward the back we have several rooms dedicated to classes like spinning, yoga and even Zumba. Thankfully someone else comes in for those since I have two left feet. A bright smile is plastered on my face every time I walk into this place.

I've been working with Clay since he opened the doors here. Before that, really. Since the day he nursed me back to the land of the living from that hangover, we've been inseparable. That is, until I met Hadley and Ryan. I have been by his side since the day that he decided to open a gym, even going so far as helping him name the place. He may not understand why I love the name so much, but he went with it. He's become a pillar in my life, an intrinsic part of my inner circle and an incredible friend.

With a smile on my face as I stride onto the floor and wave at the regular members as I pass, I walk back toward the office to put my bags away. As usual, Clay is in there on the computer, going over the schedule for next week, just like every Monday morning. His backwards baseball cap hides his messy, dark blond waves. I've noticed he always wears a baseball cap when he's at the gym. He asked me weeks ago to help with managing the place, yet he still works himself to death every freaking day. I can see the tension in his profile, his sharp jaw clenched in frustration. The ink on his muscular arms flexes as he balls up his fists, glaring at the screen.

"Babe, when are you going to trust me when I tell you I've finished the admin shit you hate?" I giggle and roll my eyes while I bend over behind him, placing my bag on the ground next to the desk.

I hear a sharp intake of breath before he scolds me, as he always does. "Jesus, Kat. You can't sneak in here like that and then be bent over when I turn around. That's just evil." He groans.

"Me, evil? Never." I wink at him before I saunter out with a bit of a bounce in my hips. The friendly, flirty banter between us is one of my favorite things about our friendship. I don't know that I would have been able to heal as much as I have since she left me had it not been for this friendship.

"I hate you," Clay calls after me.

"Lies!" I shout back at him, giggling as I walk to the front desk.

I reach the front desk where I check my classes for the day. First up is yoga, my favorite. It's a small class today. Only Hadley, Ryan, and a few more of the regulars have signed up for this one. The rest of the day looks pretty solid, though.

"Hey, Ava." I smile at the young woman, still in her first year of college, who works at the front desk for us. "Can you help me grab and re-sanitize the mats before class?"

"Sure, Kat!" She is spunky and always willing to help. She's a sweetheart and freaking gorgeous. Since she doesn't take on clients for training, she's always got a full beat of makeup on her face. The makeup accentuates her soft features making it difficult not to admire her. I'm no better than a man when I notice the athletic wear she paints on every day that accentuates her curves and slight frame.

I'm hoping that we can talk her into sticking around full time once she graduates. She's been integral in helping us streamline processes in creating class rosters and assisting us gain a more substantial following on social media.

"Thanks, babe. You're a gem!" I grin back at her as I continue on into the room off of the far end of the main floor, specifically for group classes.

We spend the next twenty minutes wiping down the yoga mats that we keep for those who haven't brought a mat or don't own their own. I see a few of the regulars coming in. The early morning classes tend to be a dumping ground of tea and drama from the local schools since most of these regulars are stay at home moms.

"Hey, Kat, what's on the agenda for today?" My least favorite student asks.

Leigh Adams, a mom of four, two sets of twins in middle and high school. She's not bad looking, she's slim, her hair is always in a messy bun like she knows no other style. She is constantly in here talking about how her babies can do no wrong, yet the other moms in the class have shared just how much trauma those kids have caused for others. It feels like the apples don't fall too far from the tree based on the gossip mill of other members.

"It's a moderate Monday." I reply cooly before turning away from the pain in my ass.

I may complain, but I do love my job. That's just one aspect of it I could do without. We're not in high school anymore, ladies. Let's act that way.

"Hey, my baby girls!" I call out as soon as I see Ryan and Hadley. "Let's get this show on the road, then we can grab coffee before my next class." I grin back at them as we take our spots among the rest of the attendees.

The class goes by in a flash, the final pose being corpse pose. Almost everyone loves it, relaxing back into the earth.

"Can't you think of a different name for that pose? It's disgusting." Leigh shouts, wrinkling her nose as she stands, leaving the borrowed mat on the ground for us to clean and put away.

Like I said, almost everyone.

"I'll take your notes into consideration, Mrs. Adams." I respond as sweetly as possible.

Sharing a look with my girls, we all walk out together, leaving Leigh behind.

The three of us walk down Marshall Avenue, coffee in hand, enjoying the warm summer weather. Though I'm the only one with an iced coffee, the two psychopaths I call my best friends drink hot coffee year round. Now that Hadley is teaching again and has Connor, she doesn't go out with us as much as she used to. Don't get me wrong, Ry and I are thrilled about her relationship with Connor because he's perfect for her, especially given her current situation. We just try to get as much time in as we can when she's around.

"So, what's new?" Hadley's voice is an octave too high.

"Not a lot for me. I'm just working and hanging out with Ry when you're not around. Which, by the way, is all the time now." I tease her.

"What about Clay? He was gawking at you again all throughout class." She grins at me with hearts in her eyes. Seriously, she's the emoji personified.

"Uh, babygirl. I think the Irishman has you confused." I roll my eyes at her.

"I don't think so. It was quite obvious today. Even *my* oblivious ass noticed it." Ryan winks at me.

"He isn't interested. Trust me, we've been friends for so long. It's just innocent flirting. That's all it's ever been." I whack Ryan's arm as I replay the morning's events in my mind.

There's no way, right?

"Whatever you say, Pickle." She smirks at me wickedly. I hate when she gets an idea like this in her head. This is precisely what happened when she made Hadley download that damn app.

"Speaking of the Irishman, how is the silver fox?" I turn my attention toward Hadley hoping to avoid continuing the conversation about Clay.

He's just a friend.

"He's great. We've been together most nights. The sex is freaking fantastic." Her cheeks tinge pink at the admission, the expression on her face says it all. "I didn't realize an orgasm could be so good."

Ry chokes on her drink. "Uh, Had, I know you and Andy have been together forever, but like. In college before he joined you?" She glances at me for backup.

"I think what she's trying to ask is, did you never have an orgasm, even self administered?" I try to stay as clinical as possible.

Hadley's face burns bright. "Andy wouldn't let me masturbate. Any time I tried to start anything over the phone, he told me he was the only one allowed to bring me pleasure." She huffs out a breath. "I thought I'd had orgasms with him, but in comparison..." She lets the words die on her tongue.

"Okay. That's it, shopping spree, on us." I announce as I pull my phone out of my pocket and send a text.

Kat:

If I'm not back by my next class at three, can you cover for me, please?

Clay:

What do I get if I do?

Kat:

Whatever you want, it's important.

Clay:

I'm going to hold you to that. I'll cover for you.

Kat:

Thanks, babe!

Chapter Two

Eminem's Without Me blares loudly from my headphones as I go through the steps I've been working on. With a few flicks of the wrist the bright red cord is whipping in such fast succession it's a blur to the untrained eye, but for me, it's one of the few things that still brings me joy. Even if only for a few minutes a day. Rope tricks are my favorite thing to do, to not only pass time, but to get the cardio out of the way. Whoever the fuck invented burpees was the goddamn devil reincarnate. Seriously, I may own a gym and I love to help people reach whatever fitness goals they wish to achieve, but some exercises are a motherfucker.

The song ends and pulls me from the zone. With a quick glance around when I stop spinning the rope, I notice a crowd. I hate when this shit happens. It's why I usually only do it when Pickle is here, my Kat. I don't know why she hates her nickname so much. It's fucking adorable. I wave everyone off as I drape the rope over my shoulders and walk to the edge of the mat to grab my water bottle. My eyes dart to the clock on the wall to check the time, I see it's ten minutes until Kat's next class. Fuck, I don't want to cover this class. It's cycling, she better not back out of the *Whatever you want to* text. What I want is a date.

Oh, calm your tits. I won't force her into anything she doesn't want to do. Consent is key No matter how much I want to show her what she means to me. I'm not a total douche canoe. No, that's her friend Hadley's husband, from what she's let slip around me. I groan, and make my way to the office to drop the rope on the desk.

When I return to the dedicated room we use for cycling, I see Leigh is here again. God, this woman. She needs a life. I'm all for fitness, obviously. But she's the most irritating person and her kids are even worse. Luckily, a few of the decent regulars are here. I smile and wave when I see them.

"Hi, ladies, good to see you." I beam.

Jenna, a blonde with a builder's body, is here along with her girlfriend Tina, who is a tiny little thing with a rainbow pixie cut. Spunky as hell, too. She gives Kat a run for her money more often than not.

"Aw, that's the most you've said to us in a month, you big ol' grump. Leigh's here, isn't she?" Tina pokes me in the ribs.

"Am I that obvious?" I chuckle as I head to the bike on the raised platform.

"Unless Kat is talking to someone and you are feeling particularly possessive in the moment, you don't bother with small talk, broseph." Tina's teasing smile causes her eyes to crinkle.

I stop where I stand, staring at her with a vacant look. "I, what?"

"Don't worry, I think she's fairly oblivious when it comes to you. You've been thoroughly friend zoned, my guy." She does something with her face that looks like she may be having a seizure.

"What the hell was that?" I ask, not bothering to respond to the friend zone comment.

"Oh, that was her wink." Jenna responds with a quiet giggle.

"Why the hell do you put your entire head into it?"

"Hey, don't judge me. I'm the one who's got a girl. You still haven't been able to land one and you *can* wink normally." Tina's sass has me frozen in my tracks.

She's not wrong.

"Well played, go get on the bike. Enjoy the payback for that comment." I wink properly at her, a sly smirk playing across my face.

Kat walks in at three forty-five, just after the class ends. Her body looks like it's built for sin with the sexy as fuck strappy pastel pink sports bra, and tight floral yoga pants that show off her curves. Her eyes are alight with mischief as she walks over to where I'm dismounting the bike.

"Hey everyone! How was class?" She's very chipper. "I'm so sorry I had to run out for a bit. I had to handle a situation. Was Clay working you all hard?"

My mouth goes dry at the comment.

"He tried to. I think he has his eyes set on working someone else harder, though." Tina winks as she and Jenna stroll out of earshot.

"That was inappropriate, Kat. You should know better. What if there were children here?" Leigh pants from her spot in the back. Sweat drips down her face.

I hold back a chuckle, seeing she's that winded from the class.

"Uh, Mrs. Adams, this is a gym for eighteen and older. There are no children here. Also, if you feel I said something inappropriate when I asked about how hard he pushed during your workout, I think that says more about where your brain was than it does mine." Kat's sweet smile is all for show, it's not the real one I've witnessed.

"You can't talk to me like that. I'm a customer!" Leigh shouts at Kat.

I step between the two.

I wrap an arm around Kat's waist and tug her behind me protectively before speaking, "Kat, office now." It comes out firm, but the way she melted into me tells me she knows it's for show. Lowering my voice when Kat disappears into the office, I look at Leigh. "You may think that you are top shit, and I'll admit that you have the ear of some of the elite in the area, but you will not speak to her that way. If you do, your membership will be revoked. Understood?"

Instead of waiting around for a response, I turn on my heel and follow in Kat's wake until I see her sitting on my chair in the office with her long legs crossed and feet resting on my desk. Her teal hair, which looks slightly faded, is in a tight ponytail showing off her high cheekbones and the cutest button nose I've ever seen. Her Persian green eyes pierce my soul when her gaze meets mine.

"She's a bitch." Kat groans as she scrubs her face with her hands..

"First off, hi. Also, yes. Additionally, you one hundred percent were being a perv and you know it!" I peel off my sweaty shirt and throw it at her.

"It's really unfair that your sweat smells good. Like, really unfair." She whines.

Chapter Three

S weat shines as it drips down the rippling muscles of his stomach. The tattoos on his skin glisten under the overhead lights and I'd be lying if I said I didn't want to lick each and every inch of his toned body. Even his sweat smells good, a woodsy scent that intoxicates my senses. But he's my friend, damnit. He's been one of my best friends for years. I shouldn't want to climb him like a freaking tree each time he works up a sweat. I try to conceal the gasp that passes my lips when he wipes himself down with a clean towel.

"So, what exactly was so important, perv?" He smirks at me, his eyes twinkling with humor.

"Oh, just something with Hadley. It's fine." My cheeks heat under his gaze.

Why am I able to openly talk about my sex life with my girls without a second thought, but with him I become an unrecognizable, shy person? How does he do this to me?

"Well, I'm glad everything is fine now. How about that repayment?" His honey-colored gaze is locked on mine.

I gulp, not knowing what to expect with the way he's staring at me.

"Sure, whatever you want." I try to smile but I'm suddenly feeling so self conscious. Clay takes a step closer to me, invading my space. The unique woodsy scent that he emits distracts me even more when he's so close. I don't hear what he says at first. "Sorry, what?"

"Go out with me tonight. You can head out early if there is anything you planned on doing after work." He grins. "No time to back out, though," with a wink, he leaves me in the office alone.

What. The. Fuck.

I watch after him, his muscular form retreating toward the free-weights where his next solo client is waiting for him. With no time to process what just happened, I realize I have an appointment with one of my clients, Aly. I see her waving at me from the elliptical where she's begun a warm up with cardio.

I cross the distance of the gym floor, doing my best not to look back at him. "Hey, babes. How are you doing today?"

As she moves on the piece of equipment, her raven locks that are pulled into a high ponytail, bounce along with her.

"I'm amazing! You'll never guess what happened to me today!" With that opening, she spends the rest of our scheduled hour telling me about how she met the love of her life, some security guy named Jax. She apparently bounced off his chest as he was exiting the Mud House and she was entering. It would be a meet cute but this woman goes on about the newest person she's falling in love with every other day. It never lasts more than a week before she's in love with someone else.

I'm flying around my apartment, trying to get myself presentable. Why the hell do I care so much when he has seen me at my literal worst? I took the time to wash and straighten my hair. I even grabbed supplies to freshen up the color on my way home. Everything that needs to be shaved, plucked, and tweezed has been. I spent an hour on my makeup, that part, though I'd expect no less. If I'm going out, I must have a full beat. After exfoliating my lips, making sure the dead skin is gone and that they are once again soft and kissable before applying my Almond Cookie liquid matte lipstick. I saw it in a video while I was doom scrolling late one night on my phone. The video showed the owner who was bubbly and relatable, so I figured I would get one. Now, I have one in every color. The first time I put it on and it didn't smudge after an entire day out with the girls which ended up at the bar, it was as though Oprah took over my body. You *get a color; you get a color, you all get a color*, but they were all for me. What can I say when you find something you like, you get it in every color. Girl math, yeah?

I send a selfie to the group chat flaunting my new low v neck T-shirt and high waisted jeans that truly enhance my ass even with the black Chuck Taylor's in place of heels. It's not until after I press send that I realize I haven't told them what's happening before now. The response is instant.

Ryan:

Damn, Pickle. You look hot. Where are you off to? I thought you were closing tonight.

Hadley:

Wow. Wait, did we have plans? I can reschedule with Connor.

Kat:

No babes, we didn't have plans. Apparently, my payment to Clay for taking my class this afternoon is to go out with him. He gave me the rest of the day off after I was with Aly to do whatever I had planned tonight.

Ryan:

I fucking knew it, Pickle! He wants you!

Hadley:

Oh my god! That's wonderful. Where are you going? What are you doing?

Kat:

Oh boy. I have no idea. I shouldn't have said anything to you two. You're going to blow this out of proportion.

Hadley:

No, we won't! We're just excited for you! You haven't really dated much since…

Ryan:

Way to go, bringing that up.

I grab an iced coffee from my fridge, popping the lid and bringing it to my mouth. Taking a long sip as they continue to go off in our text thread, I choke when I see the next message come through from Ryan.

Ryan:

Forget what Hadley said, get that dick, Pickle!

Just then, a knock on the door interrupts me from responding. I quickly lock my phone before sliding it into my back pocket. Before I cross the room, I take a deep breath to center myself. Once I reach the door I unlock the deadbolt and place my hand on the cool metal. I turn the knob and pull open the door. There before me, in a pair of light wash jeans and a Henley with a few buttons popped open, showing off his smooth muscular chest, is Clay. The sleeves are pushed up, showing off his detailed ink and forearms. It should be illegal how good this man looks.

"Hey, beautiful." His eyes rake up and down my body. "You look, damn—," his appreciative grin sends a rush of heat through me.

I giggle, teasingly thumping his chest as I step outside to join him. "You clean up pretty well too."

Chapter Four

I can't stop staring at Kat. She's always beautiful, but I rarely see her like this. All done up, her makeup is flawless. How is it possible she looks incredible, both with her face bare and covered in a sheen of sweat after a workout and with a face full of makeup?

I gently place my palm on the small of her back, the moment my hand brushes against the sliver of bare skin exposed between her shirt and jeans, my body feels more alive than it has in years. Shaking the thought from my head, I lead her from her front porch to my second favorite girl:

my Harley Fat Boy. I bought her four years ago. The bright blue body drew me in and she's such a smooth ride. Though I only added on the teal lightning bolts a couple of years ago after Kat made the change to her hair. What can I say, I've had it bad for a while.

"Where are we going?" Kat asks as I hand over her helmet.

I get myself in place on the bike while she secures her helmet. I push the kickstand back and hold my hand out to help her on. She grins, ignoring the gesture. Placing her hands on my shoulders, she climbs on, sitting so close behind me I can feel her chest rise and fall as she breathes before she scoots into place. I chuckle and I pull my own helmet on and start the bike, idling for a minute to let the engine heat back up. Once I shift into gear, we're off. Her arms wrap around my middle and hold on tightly though her hands are balled in fists instead of on me, the warm summer evening air rushes past us as we head through town.

We ride in a comfortable silence through the suburbs of Central Falls into the heavily populated Grove City, to a food truck I've been following on social media since I heard they had been traveling through the area. The schedule on their Instagram confirmed my plans as soon as she agreed to go out with me tonight. We pull into the parking lot of Lakeview Park surrounded by large trees and bright green grass, and make our way to a parking spot close to the main attraction. I can tell the instant Kat spots the truck. Her body tenses with excitement, a loud squeal can be heard even over the roar of the bike's engine.

As soon as I come to a stop, she hops off the bike and has her helmet off before I have a chance to cut the engine. Her enthusiasm is overwhelming. I chuckle as I take my helmet off. She is bouncing on her toes in front of me, a wild smile plastered across her face.

"How did you even know this existed?" She squeaks out, the excitement still rolling off in waves.

I take the helmet from her and place both of them on the bike handles.

I grab the blanket and water bottles out of my saddlebag before taking her hand and leading her toward the large pickle shaped food truck with such an appropriate name, *Quite the Pickle.*

"I keep an eye out for food trucks," I shrug, wrapping an arm around her shoulder. "Just in case."

"I can't believe you!" She pulls away, only to grab my hand and drag me behind her to get a better look at the menu.

We stand together and I chuckle enjoying the way her face lights up while she reads the menu. We get to the window and place our order. Two orders of fried pickle spears, bacon wrapped pickles, garlic and dill pickle chicken, and a couple of pickle cupcakes for dessert.

Kat's love of pickles is one of the most endearing things about her. When I met her back in college, the first thing I learned when she sobered up after getting dumped was her love of pickles. She withheld any details of the ex, which was likely for the best. I've been protective of this woman since the day we met. If she's ever had a rough day, forget the flowers. A jar of her favorite pickles, Wickles Dirty Dill Spears in case you were curious, is the only way to go.

With her hand in mine, I lead her to the side of the truck while we wait for our food.

"I can't believe you did this." She looks beautiful. She always looks beautiful, but the expression of joy on her face is breathtaking.

"I would do more than this for you, Pickle." I wink at her.

"Ugh, don't ruin the moment." She playfully thwacks my chest again with a slight smirk, pulling at the corners of her lips.

"I can tell by the spark in your eyes you don't mind when I call you Pickle." I softly caress her cheek with my thumb, her breath hitches so softly I barely hear it.

"Number 723." The cashier calls from the order window, "Your order is up!"

Reluctantly, I release her and walk over to grab our bag of food. When I turn back to her, she has a serene smile as she watches me. With the blanket still tucked under my arm, I switch the food to that hand before placing my free hand on the small of Kat's back again. Once I lead her to a grassy area near the water, we stop and spread the blanket on the ground. It takes a few moments to lie out our pickle buffet, but the way her eyes shine with glee as she takes in the assortment is comical.

"So, what was the emergency I have to thank Hadley for?" I quirk a brow as she lifts a fried pickle spear to her lips.

"Uh, let's just say Andy is even more of a douche canoe than we knew." She takes a bite, softly moaning around the pickle.

My dick strains against my jeans at the sound. I groan, attempting to subtly adjust myself while continuing to hold a conversation. "Is she ok?"

"Oh yeah, it wasn't that kind of emergency." She shrugs, "I, um, I'm not sure she'd want me to go into detail."

"Well, now I'm even more interested. I'll ask her the next time she's at the gym." I grin, grabbing a spear for myself.

"No! She would die!" Kat's cheeks tinge pink. "We took her to Sinful Secrets."

I stare at her. My eyes must show a mischievous glint because, somehow, her face and neck redden to the hue of a maraschino cherry. I open a bottle of water I had wrapped in the blanket, taking a long sip before I make a comment. Kat's eyes widen, like she knows what I'm about to say.

"And, what did *you* buy during this emergency trip?" I grin as the question passes my lips.

Chapter Five

My face is on fire as Clay looks at me, my body feels so hot that I could die right here and turn into a pile of ash. My eyes lock on him as I attempt to ignore how well he knows me.

"It was a trip for her, not me." I take another bite of the fried pickle spears I've been savoring during this conversation.

"For as long as I've known you. If you've gone shopping no matter who it was for, you always end up coming home with something for yourself." His wicked grin is giving me feelings that, if I'm honest, I've been avoiding for years now. After losing the person I was head over heels for, relationships haven't been a priority for me. The idea of losing my best friend because I couldn't keep my feelings under wraps makes my heart hurt. Relationships always end and people always leave.

"These fried pickles are so good; I can't wait to try the rest." I muse, endeavoring to change the subject.

He chuckles, handing me a bacon wrapped pickle with a wink. "I can wait to find out."

The rest of the evening goes off without a hitch, no more embarrassing topics of what sex toys I purchased. We chat about everything we usually do but, this time it feels more intimate. I've never been one for fancy dinners or expensive dates. This has been a kind of perfect that I haven't experienced since college. I shudder as memories of my ex girlfriend return with a vengeance. Clay notices the shift and pulls a hoodie he had wrapped in the blanket over my head before wrapping an arm around me.

"Kat." He whispers in my ear as we watch the sun fading beyond the horizon in the distance.

"Hmm?" I glance over at him. He has an expression in his beautiful golden eyes that makes my body want to melt into him.

"Can we try this?" he lifts a hand back to my face, lightly caressing my cheek again with his thumb. His hand moves to cup my neck as he stares into my soul.

I've known Clay for six years. He's been a constant in my life since she left me. As much as I've been fighting my feelings for him, I don't know if I can overcome the fear that is deeply rooted inside my heart.

"Clay, I —" I swallow hard as his eyes implore me to say yes. "I'm afraid of losing you, too." I admit, memories of my parents and sister flash through my mind.

"Kat, I've been at your side, what, forever now? Don't think you can get rid of me that easily." He teases, a desperate attempt to lighten the mood. He leans in, pressing a soft kiss to my forehead before continuing. "I know you've been feeling the shift between us. We both want this. What's the harm in trying?"

"What if you leave too?" I feel the tears welling in my eyes as I stare back at him.

"Princess, nothing could make me want to leave you." He holds my face between his palms, the unspoken question very clear on his face.

Taking a deep breath, I push back all of my fears. I lean into him and press my lips against his eager mouth. We lose ourselves in this moment. Finally, years of pent up attraction, chemistry, and longing break through the wall I've kept in place as our tongues tangle together. An explosion of heat rocks me to my core as I realize just how turned on I am. I moan into the kiss, knowing if this continues, we are going to be arrested for public indecency. I gently pull away from the kiss. We are both panting. A pained look flashes in his eyes before he masks it.

"Are you ok?" His question makes me smile, always checking in on me.

"More than ok, I promise." A smirk dances across my lips as I lean in and press a chaste kiss against his lips. "But we need to take this slow, and if that continues..." I feel the flush creep up my neck again.

His throaty chuckle has me ready to abandon my senses and jump him right here. "Fair enough. Let me get you home."

Clay stands to his feet, with his hand outstretched to help me stand from my position on the blanket. Once I place my palm against his, he pulls me up and crushes me into his hard chest. I let out a yelp, not expecting the quick movement. I grin up at him, my gaze locked onto his beautiful eyes.

Clay helps me on the bike once he's settled in place, this time when I wrap my arms around him I place my hands against his stomach. His muscles flex and I feel him take a sharp intake of breath when I press my chest against his back. I may want to take this slow but I can't help the desire I have for him. He forced open the floodgates when he kissed me tonight. The ride home ends too quickly, I'm not ready to say goodnight when he parks in front of my house.

Clay of course, being the gentleman that he is, helps me off of the bike and walks me to the door. His arm is wrapped tightly around my shoulders as he leads me to the front door. I can't help but giggle when he holds his hand out for my keys so he can unlock the deadbolt.

"Clay, I –" before I can finish my thought, his mouth is on me again. I whimper into the kiss as his tongue makes his way into my mouth, toying with my self control. One hand cups my cheek as the other grips the hair at the nape of my neck to give himself a better angle to deepen the exchange. My body melts into him and I let out a pathetic whine when he pulls away, effectively ending the moment.

"We have all the time in the world, Princess." With a wicked wink, he playfully slaps my ass and tells me to get some sleep before he walks back to his bike where he watches until I'm safely inside.

Waking up this morning after "the date to win all dates" was more of a challenge than I would have expected. I was so worked up I had a difficult time falling asleep last night and this morning I didn't fare much better.

My nerve endings were on fire from the moment he said goodnight until I finally gave in and used my new toy in the shower before work. My cheeks heat as my mind replays the memory of bringing myself to an out of this world climax just from the thought of Clay's lips on mine.

"Hey, Pickle." I startle when I realize that I've been lost in my thoughts while leaning against the front counter at Karma and groan at Ryan's use of my old nickname.

"Ry, I will literally pay you to stop using that." I plead, turning to face my friend.

"Sorry, Babe, there isn't enough money. The way your cheeks flush every time I call you Pickle, it brings me so much joy." She grins at me before wrapping me in an embrace. Her blonde hair is in a high ponytail, pulled out of her face. Her big brown eyes brim with amusement.

Oh, if she only knew what really had me blushing this morning.

"I have to take her side on this one." Clay chimes in as he swaggers past us with a wink.

"I hate you all." I pout.

"Lies!" Clay repeats my response from the other day.

"Hadley spent the night with Connor, so she won't be here, but we're meeting at Finley's tonight." Ryan grins at me, knowing we're going to get trashed as we usually do when we end up at our favorite dive bar.

"Ok. Now, go!" I point toward an elliptical, which is Ryan's least favorite machine. Her answering glare provides just as much joy for me that my nickname gives her. "Payback, babygirl." I wink at her.

I spend the next hour with her on a cardio circuit. You would think she'd learn her lesson. We may be friends, but as long as she allows me to be her personal trainer while continuing to use that dreadful name, I'll have my own fun.

I giggle as she steps off the last machine, drenched in sweat. Ryan disappears into the locker room to shower. I'm sitting at the front counter with Ava when she comes back out. We need to go over the upcoming schedule for my personal clients and classes. Ryan hardly acknowledges me by flipping me off as she strides past us.

"See you tonight, Pickle." She calls out over her shoulder as the door closes behind her.

"Damnit!" I laugh, annoyed yet amused that she got the last word.

Chapter Six

I have been paying even more attention to Kat from across the gym today than I normally do, like an absolute creep. I have been tempted so many times to pull her into a corner and kiss her. The time we shared last night wasn't remotely close to enough. I've watched as she's gone from client to client, class to class, I don't realize how obvious I've been until a client calls me out on it.

"Man, you're drooling even more than usual today. When are you going to just go for it?" One of my favorite clients who also happens to be my good friend, Johnny Lewis, slaps my shoulder as his eyes follow my gaze.

"Shut up, asshole." I chuckle, turning back to him. "Give me four reps of ten shoulder presses, you were at fifty pounds."

"As your friend, and attorney for that matter, I'm going to advise that you really do shoot your shot." Johnny lifts the dumbbells to his shoulders and begins his first set. "At this rate, I'm going to have to deal with a sexual harassment case as soon as she catches you gawking like you have been today."

"Fuck off man," I grin at him. "We went out last night."

"About fucking time! Why are you staring at her like this then?" He nods in Kat's direction "Go pull her into the office and make out, I can do my sets without you holding my damn hand."

I roll my eyes at him but take the opportunity to sneak away for a moment with my girl. She's currently at the front desk talking to Ava when I approach. Her eyes are locked on Kat who is animatedly going on about some book she finished last night. I grin as I sneak up behind them, pressing my chest against Kat's back. She stiffens until she hears my voice, melting into me.

"Office, now." I whisper into her ear, low enough for only her to hear.

I turn around and cross the distance on the floor to my office. I keep my back to the door, my hands gripping my hips when I feel her approach. I don't turn until I hear the tell-tale click of the latch, the door is closed. I've never been so happy to have a solid door and no windows in this office as I am right now.

I have her pinned against the door in the span of a singular heartbeat. My lips on hers, my hand gripping her hip, the other fisted around her ponytail. She gasps, allowing my tongue access to savor her. Her arms loop around my neck, she tosses my hat somewhere behind me as she tangles her fingers in my hair. I grind my length against her belly as my tongue continues its exploration of her mouth. Soft moans escape Kat's luscious pink lips. I pull away after another moment, knowing full well that if I continue, I won't let her out of this office until I have my fill of her. Both of us are gasping for breath when we separate.

"What was that for?" She pants.

"I needed a *Pickle* fix." I wink at her. "I couldn't wait until our next date."

"I'm glad you didn't." Kat's feisty smirk has my cock throbbing in my shorts. "Let me know when you want that second date."

"If Johnny weren't here, I'd say now." I pull her back into my chest, pressing my lips against hers again in a brief kiss.

"I'd love that, but I have plans with the girls that I actually need to leave to get ready for." Her eyes sparkle as she stares up at me, reminding me of the Caribbean Sea. But not the deep water. No, the parts closer to the shore, where the deep blues melt together with the subtle greens. A color so perfect, I could drown in her gaze.

"Call me if you need a ride. I know how the three of you get." I level her with a serious gaze. "Let me know when you're home."

"Yes, sir." She winks before opening the office door and walking back out into the gym.

The rest of my day goes by frustratingly slowly even though it was busier than usual. I barely had enough time to scarf my roasted chicken Caesar salad between clients. The time finally comes to close the gym for the night, and I get the front and back doors locked up until morning. I return to my office and head up the stairs to my connected apartment.

My cock has been at half-mast ever since the intense kiss in the office. It didn't help that as soon as she was ready to go out to see the girls, she sent me a selfie. The woman looked good enough to eat and I'm not allowed to have her on my personal menu just yet. Johnny gave me shit the rest of our session. If it were anyone else, I would have hit them. Johnny's been one of my best friends since I opened the gym. He's been aware of my feelings for Kat longer than I even have been.

My door that connects to my apartment from the office opens to a huge open concept space. My living room and kitchen are connected, the couch is the only barrier between the two designated spaces. I step into my kitchen and yank open the refrigerator door to pull out a beer. I use the counter to pop the top off. Taking a long pull, I savor the feel of the cold crisp liquid as it courses through my body. The way the bubbles tickle my nose with each sip keeps a smile on my face.

I cross the open space into my living room and take a seat on my couch before I turn on the TV. Luckily for me, my favorite movie, Boondock Saints just started on whatever channel was last on. I settle in for the night ready to enjoy the movie when my phone vibrates in my hand with a text.

Pickle:

I'm home, Sir. (winky emoji)

Clay:

Kat, behave. I'm glad you're home safe.

Pickle:

You're no fun.

Clay:

Go out with me tomorrow and I'll show you how much fun I can be.

Pickle:

It's a date. Where are we going?

Clay:

It's a surprise.

Pickle:

How am I supposed to dress for surprise?

Clay:

You know that purple dress with the yellow flowers that you wore in the pictures Ryan took of you at the waterfall?

Pickle:

Should I be impressed or concerned that you know what I was wearing during the last shoot?

Clay:

Impressed that I pay attention? Yes. Concerned with how many times I imagined that dress on my bedroom floor? Probably.

Pickle:

I thought we were behaving?

Clay:

We are, I'm just answering your question. (winky emoji)

Goodnight, beautiful. See you tomorrow.

Chapter Seven

We've been sitting at our table at Finley's for two hours. We've gotten every appetizer on the menu and are on our second round of drinks. I'm not sure what comes over me when I decide to make an announcement.

"I think I'm going to sleep with Clay." Lifting my drink, I take a generous sip as I watch Hadley and Ryan for their reaction. They share a look I can't quite decipher.

"The owner of your gym, Clay?" Ryan's question is filled with amusement.

"Yep. He's been hinting that he wants to take me out for months and, well, I think I'm going to sleep with him." I declare with more confidence than I feel. Knowing damn well I've been hiding behind my delusions that this wasn't what was happening.

They know we went out last night but I haven't gone into the details of what happened. I smirk at the memories of our pickle date.

"It's about damn time, woman!" Ryan and Hadley say in unison.

"Seriously? Am I that obvious?" I reply coyly.

"Listen, babes, Had and I have been waiting for you to take the plunge for a while. He's a good place to start." Ryan pauses, a careful look taking hold of her features. "I know Anya fucked you up, bit it's been a long-ass time for you to not be interested in anyone. If you're attracted to him, get that dick, Pickle!" Her voice rises with growing excitement.

Oh my god. She did not just say that! I feel my cheeks heating as I glance over to Hadley. Silently begging for her to save me. I've known Hadley a little longer than Ryan and the two of us just clicked. She gets me, even if Ryan and I have hooked up in the past, it's Hadley that has kept me sane throughout the years we've known each other.

"On that note, I think we've had enough to drink." Hadley's giggle is infectious.

Texting back and forth with Clay when I get home makes me happier than I care to admit. It's not until the final text, *Good night, beautiful* that has my smile morphing into a Cheshire grin. I haven't felt this giddy since –. No, I will not think about her.

I change out of my black strappy mini dress into a long T-shirt and climb into bed. I can't help but think of what Clay has in store for us tomorrow after work. In an attempt to distract myself from what his plans may be, I doom scroll through the video app on my phone for a while before sleep finally finds me.

It's been a gloomy day, a storm has been rolling through since sometime after I fell asleep last night. The gym has been dead, one or two members coming in, but everyone canceled their attendance to the one on one training. No one showed up for the classes. I collapse next to Ava behind the front desk.

"I hate rainy days, no one wants to go out." I pout.

"It's coming down pretty bad. They're calling for flooding in Ellicott City." She bats her eyelashes at me.

"Go home, babe. Be safe, we can keep the crowds under control for the day." I snort.

"Thanks, Kat." Ava's smile is so bright, she leans in and wraps her arms around my shoulders. "Have a good night."

"See ya," I pat her on the back with a friendly wave as she walks away.

Looking around the empty gym, I smile to myself as I wander toward the office where I find Clay with his feet up on his desk and his black baseball cap laying on his face, covering his eyes. The purple Karma Gym

T-shirt is pulled taut over his broad chest. I lean against the doorframe for a moment, watching him.

"You're being a creep right now." His voice startles me so badly I jump, my elbow hitting the doorframe.

"Son of a," I start as I hold my arm, trying to massage out the pain. "I don't understand why people call this a funny bone, it is decidedly not funny when you hit it."

His throaty chuckle pulls my gaze back toward him. "Sorry, you're not as stealthy as you think, I couldn't resist."

He sits up, placing his feet on the floor. A charming smile pulls at his lips as he keeps his eyes locked on me. I feel so shy under his honey colored gaze, how the hell am I going to go through with what I told Ryan and Hadley last night?

"I sent Ava home, they're calling for flooding in Ellicott City. I didn't want her to risk it when we've been dead most of the day anyways." I shrug. "I'm going to get a shower, we can reschedule whatever you had planned since the weather is so bad."

Clay arches a brow at me as I turn toward the locker room for a shower. I feel his strong hand around the delicate skin of my wrist, I gasp as he pushes me against the closed door that leads from the office to his apartment. His mouth crashes against mine, his tongue passes my lips. My hands fist his hair, no longer able to control myself. I do in fact climb him like a tree. My legs wrap around his waist and I cling onto him as if it's a matter of life or death. His strong arms cage me against his chest, I can feel the muscles ripple under his shirt.

"Or, you can just stay here and we can watch the new seasons of *Drag Race*, because I know that if you go home right now that's what you're going to do." He says after pulling away from the kiss. "That way I can at least feel you against me for longer."

"You know you're a fan of the show too." I grin at him, amused at how well he knows me. My body is still humming from the sensation of his hard chest against mine, his huge arms caging me in.

"I'm a fan of anything that keeps you close to me." He winks before releasing me and playfully slapping my ass before walking away. "You can shower down here or upstairs, I'm going to close up early."

Chapter Eight

After locking both gym entrances, I shut off the main lights and leave only the security lights on overnight. The streets are empty as I watch the rain through the large windows at the front of the gym for a few minutes. The clouds are dark in the sky, and it's an ominous sight. Ready to put a positive foot forward, I make my return to the office and climb the steps to my apartment. It's a large space, taking up the entire length of the gym downstairs.

The entrance from my office leads into the kitchen. I cross the distance to my fridge and pull out something to cook for us for dinner. My body feels too warm and overdressed, so I peel my T-shirt over my head and toss it behind me. I hear a shriek, so I spin to see Kat wrapped in a towel and my discarded T-shirt covering her face.

"I was going to ask for a clean shirt, but I can make this work." She laughs, pulling the shirt off of her face.

My god, seeing her in swimsuits over the years has nothing on seeing her dripping wet with a towel wrapped around her in my goddamn kitchen. My mouth went dry as soon as my gaze landed on her, at a complete loss for words for longer than necessary. Fuck me, she's stunning, her hair is still pulled back into a ponytail, her face is fresh and bare of makeup. Her cheeks are full of color like she's anticipating tonight as much as I am.

"You are too fucking beautiful." I groan, holding my hand out for her to come closer. With a shy smile she places her palm in mine before I pull her flush against my bare chest.

"Eek!" A quiet squeak escapes her as I hold her close with one arm, the other cupping her cheek as I stare down into the depths of her radiant eyes.

My mouth is on hers, her lips become pliant as my tongue swipes against her, eager to claim her once again. Toned arms loop around my neck once again as her breasts mold to the contours of my chest. She fists my hair, deepening the kiss. Soft whimpers escape into my mouth only making my already stiffening length even harder. The waistband of my pants digs into my cock. I nip at her bottom lip once before pulling away.

"Please let me be around for every shower you have in the future. Jesus, fuck, Kat." With my forehead pressed against hers, I tangle my fingers with Kat's and lead her to my room. I pull out my favorite band tee. Pop Evil displayed proudly at the top with a pink guitar in the center of purple iridescent angel wings spanning across the front. The stems of roses wrapped around the body and neck of the instrument brings even more to the design. As soon as she sees the shirt, which she has tried to steal more often than not, her face turns into a wicked grin.

"Does this mean I can keep it now?" She asks.

"You can wear it whenever you come over, I'm not quite ready to give it up completely," I wink at her with a smirk pulling on my lips, "yet."

Kat subtly shakes her head with a quiet laugh as she takes the shirt from me. I turn to leave the room before she drops the towel. While consent is key, I've wanted this woman for so long. Just the knowledge that we're getting closer, I don't have enough willpower to hold myself back from taking her if I see what is under that towel.

She takes her time in my room while I throw together some chicken, peppers, and onions in a pan. I dig through my fridge in search of the container of guacamole while the meat and vegetables cook on the stove. Just as I stand back to my full height I hear a thud behind me. My heart stutters in my chest, adrenaline coursing through my veins. I spin on my heels to see Kat sitting on the counter watching me, her bare legs crossed in front of her. The corners of her mouth twitch when she catches the way my eyes rake up and down her body. She's wearing my shirt with no fucking bra; her nipples are pebbled under the fabric. Jesus Christ.

"What ya making?" Her tone is innocent and playful. It's not like we've never done this before. This time it's different. Even if she changed into my clothes over the years, she didn't forgo the pants.

"Kat," I groan out her name as I cross the width of the room to crowd her space. Placing my palms on the counter on either side of her hips, I press my lips against her forehead. She grips my nape, digging her nails into my flesh as she pulls me down to meet her lips. She unhooks her legs, spreading herself for me.

"Clay, please." She pants, her mouth trailing kisses along my jaw. Her feet hook around my waist pulling me into her.

"Are you sure?" My self-control is wavering with every beat.

A whimper passes her lips as I grind my length against her heat. Moving my hands to her thighs, lifting the shirt enough to grab her hips, I find she's wearing the tiniest thong ever made. I groan again, my face drops to her neck. I nip the sensitive skin where her neck and shoulder connect, as my fingers dig into the warm flesh of her firm ass.

"Yes." If my face wasn't still buried in her neck, I wouldn't have heard it.

I raise my head, staring into the depths of her soulful eyes. When I see the desire that matches my own within her eyes, I grin for a moment as I take in the sight before me. My lips press against hers again briefly before I pull her closer to the edge of the counter. Pulling myself away from her, I smirk to myself when she whines again. I kneel before her and drag her thong down her long, luscious legs to expose her center. I lean in, bringing my face closer to core. Kat's gasp when my scruff scratches against her sensitive skin makes my cock twitch. I place her legs over my shoulders before I lean in and blow a breath of warm air along the length of her pussy. She's panting in need by the time I reach her clit.

I inhale the sweet scent of her arousal, it's intoxicating. My tongue swipes along the apex of her thighs before I reach her clit and latch on swirling tight circles around the sensitive bundle of nerves. Her sweet tangy flavor explodes on my taste buds. Soft whimpers escape as I devour her. I part her puffy pink lips with one hand before fucking her with my tongue. My eyes are locked on her face, the lights flicker just before the power goes out entirely. She cries out in agony as she climbs closer to her climax, needing the release. I chuckle against her core before removing my tongue, I slide a thick finger inside her. A soft hiss at the intrusion is the only verbal response I get. She's so fucking tight, my cock is weeping wanting to feel her, to claim her. I draw her sensitive bundle of nerves between my lips as I add a second finger, finding the most sensitive spot inside her. I make it my mission to drag the orgasm out of her, she arches her back as her pussy clenches around my fingers. Kat's hands are in my hair as she writhes against my face.

"Oh god! Clay!" She cries out as her legs begin to tremble around my neck. "I'm," Her eyes go wide, "...fire!"

Fire? The fuck.

I move away from her when I notice a glow coming from behind me. My body is so heated from my own arousal, I didn't notice when the flames started. Standing quickly, I wrap my arm around her middle carrying her with me so she doesn't collapse on weak legs. I smother the flames that have started in the long forgotten fajitas fixings with the lid to a pan. Carefully turning off the flame, *fucking gas stoves*. I remove the pan from the burner allowing it to cool down before I try to clean it out. Kat's giggling in my arm, her hands looped around my neck as I drag her around the room with me.

"Are you ok?" Arching a brow at her.

"I'm more than ok." She continues giggling, "I just finally understand why Paris Hilton says, *That's hot.*" She's snorting at her own joke.

Chapter Nine

The organ in my chest is beating against my ribs like a snare drum. The mind-blowing orgasm has my knees wobbly and my bones have turned to Jello. Even with the people I've fooled around with in the past, no man has ever been able to do that. Usually only a woman can work me over like this, making my soul leave my body from the earth-shattering pleasure.

"Is it a good sign that we started a fire the first time that we messed around or a bad omen?" I giggle, my arms still looped around his neck as a mischievous grin is tugging at the corners of his lips.

"Princess, I can still feel your legs tremble. Nothing about what just happened is a bad omen." He leans in to kiss me once again nipping at my lips until they part in a gasp, his tongue teasing mine. The taste of myself on his lips is so erotic. I moan into him as he deepens the kiss, claiming my mouth. It leaves no question as to who I belong to.

The lights flicker back on, illuminating the kitchen in brightness. I flinch and bury my face into Clay's neck at the shock to my retinas. His arms tighten around me once more, I breathe in his woodsy scent and melt even further into him.

"How about I order a pizza?" His question makes me laugh knowing he's as distracted as I am in his presence.

"Genova's," we say simultaneously, an amused look passes between us before he pulls his cell out of his pocket and makes the call.

Once the order is placed, I lace my fingers with his and pull him over to the couch. We sit down, his arms wrap around me as I turn the TV on. Before I can press play on the newest season of *RuPaul's Drag Race* I turn in Clay's arms to face him.

"I want to tell you something that I don't think we've talked about before." Before I continue, I take a deep breath as I try to calm my nerves, "I've never actually had sex with a guy." My cheeks flush bright red at the admission. Unable to meet his gaze, I keep my eyes locked on his gloriously sculpted chest.

"What? But you've dated people since we've known each other." His voice is laced with confusion.

"I've messed around with guys." I begin, trying to find the words, "I've slept with women, a lot of women. With men, it's only been oral and some hand stuff. I've never felt comfortable enough going further."

"Is this your way of telling me you're putting me back in the friend-zone?" The apprehension in his tone drags me out of my own anxieties.

"What, no." I shake my head and raise my gaze to meet his. "I'm telling you that while I may not technically be a *virgin* because strap-ons are a fun time. I think I'd like you to be my first. I mean. When we get there. Not to say I'm going to jump you right now. Unless, I mean." I stutter over my words unsure of what I'm even ready for.

"Hey, no. Princess. I didn't devour your perfect little cunt tonight for any reason other than to see the pure bliss on your face after." His cocky grin has a smile forming on my own face. "We don't have to do anything else until you're ready."

My face splits into a grin at his understanding, I plaster my front to his chest as I crash my lips to his. I shouldn't be surprised at my hesitation. The last time I even messed around with a guy was about a year after she left me. I've always been mostly attracted to women. Some men do it for me, Clay especially, which I will never admit in front of Ryan. She'll never let me live it down with as much as she's been pushing this since we decided to end the benefits part of our friendship. She's constantly insisted that there was something more between Clay and I from the day she and I met.

I pull away from him, my gaze locked on his face taking him in. He looks amused and at peace. The twitch of his lips quickly turns into a charming smile that he can't fight and it has me erupting into a fit of giggles. Before any further thoughts can form in my mind, I'm lifted to my feet. Clay stands and looms over me like a gorgeous god made of pure muscle. He links our fingers together before tugging me behind him.

"What are…?" I start one question only to finish with a different one, "where are we going?"

I hear a deep chuckle come from him as he's still dragging me behind him. In no time at all we stand in front of a door I haven't seen before. Though when I've been in his apartment many times before it's mostly been in the kitchen or living room. Occasionally the bathroom if I had to pee but even then I didn't snoop. I've never wanted to invade his privacy. I think in the back of my mind I knew if I found out another woman had been in his space it would break me.

I'm definitely not telling Ryan that.

"There is something you mentioned once you wanted to do but never have, so, I'm going to make that happen. Now." Clay's confidence in this moment is sexy as fucking hell.

I continue to follow behind as he turns the knob and presses his hand against the solid wood door to open it. A narrow staircase leads up to another door. He grips my hand tighter, not letting me out of this odd situation I've landed myself in. I follow him up the steps into the unknown only to be led to another door he opens to the roof, rain still pouring from the threatening storm clouds high in the sky.

"Clay, what?" I stare at him in confusion. A lump forming in my throat as a memory from a conversation long ago replays in my mind.

My back against the couch cushions as tears fall from my eyes. My face is still flush from the constant tears I've shed since she left me. Clay sits comfortably next to me, his arm around my shoulders to keep me from completely crumbling. We're watching One Tree Hill, Nathan and Haley are kissing in front of her house after putting their feelings out there once

Nathan apologizes for being an idiot and they finally become officially official.

"I want that, someone to consume me and claim me in the rain. It's just so, so...." I sigh, "romantic."

"I've wanted to do this since you made that comment not long after we met, but I knew you weren't ready." He smirks as he pulls me into his chest.

Chapter Ten

Seeing Kat stand here in the rain, her eyes shining with tears while she has the biggest smile on her face makes my cock pulse in my pants. She's so fucking stunning and this scenario only adds to her beauty. I cup her neck, pulling her flush against my chest. Her breasts are pressed into me so close I can feel her peaked nipples through my shirt. I smirk at her, knowing what she's waiting for me to crash my mouth against hers.

Tongues and teeth clash together in a heated messy kiss that takes our breaths away. I lift her into my arms, my hands cupping her exquisite ass.

Kat instinctively wraps her legs around me as I carry her back through the door and down the steps into my apartment. Her mouth presses kisses against my slick skin from my lips trailing down my jaw and neck. My cock strains against my shorts.

Fuck.

I crash into the textured edges of the wall and pin her against the wall. She giggles and moans simultaneously when she feels my length grinding against her center. I groan into her neck at the delicious friction. She clings onto me like a koala when I attempt to set her down, she whimpers as if the idea of not being connected to me is painful.

"Princess, a man only has so much self-control, if you want to take this slow, I need a minute." It comes out in a pained groan.

"Please. I need you." She begs so beautifully.

I pull back quickly, staring into her eyes. There can be no doubt, she has to be completely ready for this. A sly smirk tugs at my lips when I see the lust, the need in her beautiful sea green eyes. Our lips meet again as I carry her down the hall to my room. Not stopping until I finally reach my bed. I lay her down gently before standing back up to take her in.

"You're so fucking beautiful, Princess." I breathe.

Kat's face is flush, her eyes hooded. She squirms under my gaze. I lean down, pressing my lips to hers, curling my fingers under the hem of my soaked shirt clinging to the contours of her luscious body and slowly lifting it over her head before I toss the shirt somewhere behind me. Essentially, exposing her entire body to me in one fluid motion. I groan as I take her in. She's fucking gorgeous. Perfect. Before I can make a move to rid myself of my pants she pops up sitting in front of me. Her eyes stare up at my body. She parts her lips, ready to speak, but nothing comes out. Arching a brow, I cup her cheek with a hand.

"What is it?" My voice is soft, a heady need to know what's going on in that pretty little head of hers.

"I need to taste you." Her admission comes out almost as a moan and Jesus fucking Christ, she's going to kill me, and I'm going to beg her for more.

"Take what you want, Kat. I'm yours." I grin at her, staying still so she has all the control.

She doesn't take her eyes off me as she hooks her fingers under the waistband of my pants, and tugs them down over my hips. My cock springs free, nearly whacking her in the face. It doesn't deter her, if anything it just makes her intent even more clear. She smirks in a devilish way I've never seen on her, and *MY GOD* I may explode from that look alone.

I lock my hands together behind my back as she licks her lips and then leans forward. Her eyes are still locked on me, never leaving my face. She wraps her pink pouty lips around the head of my dick, sucking like it's a fucking lollipop. Kat's hands are on my thighs as she takes me further into her throat. My head rolls back onto my shoulders as the pleasure becomes too much. A guttural groan escapes as my soul tries to leave my body. I've been wanting this, wanting her, for so long.

"Baby, if you don't stop, I'm going to come, and as much as I want to fill your throat, I need to feel your pussy." I admit through staggered breaths.

I regain control of my neck as she pulls back one last time, an audible pop sounds as she releases my cock. Bending down, I crash my lips against hers. Guiding her back onto the bed, I pull away to grab a condom from my nightstand. She smiles shyly at me as I loom over her.

"I know you're not technically a virgin, but I'm still gonna take it slow. Alright?" I can see the nerves; it's written so clearly across her face. She may have used toys with her ex-girlfriend, and by herself, but this is a big step.

"Yes," her response is so soft, but I hear it.

I bring the foil package up to my mouth, tearing it open with my teeth. Once I have the condom rolled down my shaft, I lower myself one more time, tasting the sweetness between her legs. She cries out in pleasure when she feels my tongue swipe against her center.

"Clay! Please!" She's whimpering, so fucking needy.

Climbing back up her body, I kiss her again as I notch myself at her entrance. Kat's legs are hooked around my waist, her feet digging into my ass trying to pull me closer. I chuckle darkly as I slide inside her. We both moan at the sensation. She's so fucking tight my eyes nearly roll to the back of my head. It takes everything inside me to keep my eyes open to be able to gauge her reaction. The expression on her face is breathtaking. She pleads with me to move with her eyes. I slide slowly inch by inch giving her enough time to adjust to me. Once I'm fully seated inside her, she tightens around me.

"Fuck, Baby." I groan at the sensation.

I know I'm not going to be able to last. I thought her mouth was perfect. Goddamn, nothing can compare to the feel of being inside her. I start to move, thrusting in and out of her. The look of bliss on her face has my dick weeping inside her. I feel the pleasure as it builds at the base of my spine, my balls tighten with each movement. I bring my hand between us, pinching her clit as I pound harder into her. She screams out as her cunt tightens, convulsing around me. The sensation sends me over the edge as I find my release with her.

Chapter Eleven

I t's been three weeks since Clay and I have taken the plunge, fully committing to one another. A whirlwind of emotions constantly rushes through me every time I'm with him. I never expected to have this with anyone. Not after she left the way she did. It's incredible having this connection. I understand why Hadley is so obsessed with Connor. I just wish she would leave Andy once and for all. She deserves the happiness he gives her constantly, not just part time.

A few days ago, I went to her house and found her bloody and bruised. He had hit her. The motherfucker hit her. I don't know how long it's been going on. She wouldn't talk to me about it. Ryan came over and we tried to talk her into coming with us. She wouldn't leave him. Even after he hurt her, she wouldn't leave him.

Anger heats in my veins as the memory of her looking so broken comes to the front of my mind. When Ryan and I left her after that, we went to Finley's to day drink. It seemed like the only way to cope with what we had witnessed. Connor asked us to keep her safe and we tried, but what else can we do when she won't accept our help?

I'm lying in bed with Clay while an episode of *RuPaul's Drag Race All Stars* streams on the television screen. He's playing with my hair; it's so relaxing I start to doze off. I close my eyes as Angie picks Vanjie to be her teammate for the real estate challenge when my phone dings with a text notification.

Hadley:

> I don't know where to start. I'm sorry for what you've been forced to endure with me over the past months. We've been friends for years and I will be forever grateful but this pain has become too much. There is only one way to make it stop. I know that now. At least it's only a matter of time now. Tell Connor I'm sorry for bringing my mess into his life and I loved him more than I thought I could ever love anyone.
>
> I love you both so much.
>
> Take care of each other.
>
> xx
>
> Had

My heart thuds in my chest and begins to beat even harder when I realize what I'm reading. "What the fuck." I leap out of Clay's embrace and race down the stairs to his office and rush out the front door, barely stopping to grab my keys.

I don't bother looking back to Clay, as soon as I get into my car and am driving to her house my phone rings. I don't bother looking, I know who it is. I press the answer button on the steering wheel before I speak.

"I'm on my way. I got it. She wouldn't do this. She couldn't." I sob into the phone, taking a turn a little too hard and feel the passenger side of my car rise off of the ground. "Shit!"

"Jesus, woman. Are you ok?" Ryan shrieks into the phone.

"I'm fine, I took a turn too hard." Taking a deep breath before continuing, "How far away are you?"

"I'm only five minutes from her. I was at the studio. Where are you?"

"I was at Clay's. I'll meet you there in five." Pressing the end button on the steering wheel I disconnect the call.

I press the call button once more time and instruct the hands free system, "Call nine one one."

I'm still on the phone with the emergency dispatch operator when I pull up to Hadley's house. As soon as my door is open and my feet are on the ground, I hear Ryan pulling up behind me, her tires screeching to a halt right behind my car. Her door swings open, she's bouncing up the walkway behind me.

"Please stay on the line until the first responders are on the scene ma'am." The gentle soul on the other side of the line recites a line that I half expected to sound robotic with as many times as they've likely had to repeat it on a daily basis.

"Ok. We're going in though." I say, not bothering to listen to what the person on the other end of the phone says in response.

We enter the house and immediately split up to call for Hadley. There's no answer, when I return to the foyer, Ryan and I share a look before we turn toward the steps. I climb the stairs, taking two at a time, thanking the heavens above that it wasn't leg day. I race to the bathroom, where I hear Avenged Sevenfold playing. When I reach the door, I scream at the sight before me. Hadley is laying in the tub; fresh blood is pooling around her. I can see the gashes in her wrists. My past and present flash before me.

"Hadley, baby, wake up! Come back to us!" I cry out as I drop to my knees beside her. I place the phone on the ground and grab the towels hanging from the rack attached to the wall.

Ryan comes up behind me after what feels like forever, "goddamn it, Hadley, don't fucking do this." The sobs are wrecking through her, it's so unlike the woman I've known for the past six years.

When the paramedics arrive, the operator finally allows the call to disconnect. I pull Ryan back to allow the medics space to get to Hadley's side. Once they have her stable enough to move, a transfer board appears, and she's loaded on. Ry and I follow them down the steps all the way to the ambulance.

"Ladies, you can't get in the rig. You can follow us and meet us there." An older gentleman in uniform relays to us as they load her onto a gurney.

"Sir, if you think for one fucking second you are going to get us to leave our sister you can suck my strap-on because there is no way in hell we're not going to be by her side until we know she's ok." I snarl at him.

He looks appalled, but he steps aside allowing us to sit with her on the way to the hospital.

"Suck my strap-on?" Ryan laughs through her tears.

"Yea, well. It was the first thing that came to mind." I sniff, holding back my emotions so I don't blubber in front of the medics.

Clay:

How is she?

Kat:

We don't know. They put her in a medically induced coma, they had to give her a blood transfusion because of how much she's lost. It's bad. It's really bad. The internal injuries alone, she may not wake up.

Clay:

Are you sure you don't need me there, Princess?

Kat:

I need you but they won't let anyone else in the room.

"Hadley Veronica James, I swear to God. If you don't wake up, I will never forgive you." I look up from my phone to see Ryan pacing back and forth at Hadley's bedside.

"Ryan, shut up. Let her wake up before you yell at her," I whisper-shout at her.

"Fuck that. I can't yell at her when she wakes up, Pickle," Ryan groans.

I grab hold of Hadley's hand that's closest to me and squeeze.

"Come back to us, baby. We'll kill each other without you." It's barely a whisper, but I know she hears me. I lean down close to her ear before I start to sing, it may be a quiet jumbled murmur of a song, but I'm sure she knows the words I'm serenading her with. Pausing for a moment, when my voice begins to shake. "Or something like that. Hakuna matata. Come back to us, baby."

A soft knock pulls our attention away from Hadley. I look up toward the door to find the most glorious sight to have ever existed. Clay is standing there in a tank top showing off his muscular ink covered arms holding good coffee, not the shit the hospital claims is coffee.

"What are you doing here?" I gently release Hadley's hand, jumping to my feet and closing the distance between us. Looping my arms around his neck, I breathe in his intoxicating masculine scent. The familiarity of his arms and his scent has an instant calming effect on me.

"I know they won't let me stay for long, but I wanted to check on you both." His smile is sad as he glances over me at Hadley's still form. He wraps his arms around my middle, holding me tight against him.

"Thank you." I quietly cry into his neck.

I feel him move, presumably putting down the coffee. Suddenly Ryan is next to me, wrapped around both of us. I don't think I would be able to keep it together even remotely as well as I am without these two.

It's been the longest week of my life waiting and watching for any sign that Hadley will survive this. Ryan and I have been ready to throw each other out the window several times over the past few days. And this is why our friends with benefits arrangement ended, we become toxic when sex is involved.

I remember smiling at Ryan's sleeping form before I lay my head down on Hadley's legs to rest my eyes for just a few moments. When I'm jolted awake by shrill screams of someone begging for help. I bolt upright to see Hadley's eyes wide and frantic with worry. Over the next hour, nurses and doctors are in and out checking on Hadley, her vitals, and going over what has happened in the last week.

When the charge nurse, Lily, is finally done speaking to Hadley, she leaves the room. Ry and I are holding one another's hands as we stare down at our friend. I have tears streaming down my face, and I can hear Ryan's soft sobs just a second before she lunges at Hadley.

"Oh my god, you're going to hurt her, you crazy ass!" I scold!

"It's ok. I deserve it." Hadley's voice is so soft as she wraps her arms around Ryan's tiny form. "I'm so sorry. I know I've already said it, but I am so freaking sorry."

"We're just glad you're ok, baby." My response is a breathy sob.

"The one time I talked to my family about leaving, they made me feel so guilty. It was my fault he wanted Naomi. My fault that he was hurting me. I was so embarrassed and anxious over disappointing them or anyone finding out that I wasn't good enough to keep him…"

"Fuck Andy." Ryan and I say in unison.

Hadley holds her hand out to me, and I go to her, wrapping my arms around both of my friends. I bury my face into her neck as the gut wrenching thoughts of the possibility of losing her and now knowing she will be okay consume me. We stay wrapped up in each other for a while before Hadley finally pushes us away.

"I love you both, but go home, shower. You're starting to smell." She wrinkles her nose up, making a face, all the while trying not to laugh.

"Asshole!" Ry's giggle is infectious as she playfully but gently shoves Hadley back to the bed before her face turns serious. "We're not leaving you though. So, don't bother trying to get rid of us."

"Yea, absolutely not. We're here for the duration of your stay." I nod in agreement.

"Ok but both of you don't have to stay, why don't you go shower and take a nap in your own bed and then come back later and switch off." Hadley's eyes are on me, her voice sounds hopeful for the first time since the abuse started. "I promise you; I'm not going anywhere."

I share a look with Ryan before I turn back to Hadley.

"Ok, but if you even think about taking a nosedive, I'll bring you back just to fight you." I glare at her, but a smile pulls at my lips.

I pull my phone out of my pocket to see several missed calls and texts, some from Clay. but also some from a number I don't recognize.

I open the message from the unknown number and stop in my tracks.

Unknown:

> Howya, It's Alannah, Connor's sister. I snagged your info from his phone.

Kat:

> Hi, Is everything ok?

Alannah:

> He's a wreck, can we chat?

I glance over my shoulder toward the room where my two best friends remain.

Kat:

> Sure, but understand, I can't divulge specifics. Her story isn't mine to tell but she has too much healing to do. She isn't ready to see him yet.

After texting back and forth for a while longer, Alannah said she would tell Connor what I shared. She isn't happy that I won't give any further information, but she's not fighting me on it, so thank god for that.

Chapter Twelve

I glance around the old dive bar as I sit next to Johnny while we shoot the shit. My stomach has been in my ass for over a week. Kat's been at Hadley's bedside since they found her. I wouldn't expect any less but she and Ryan are burning the candle at both ends and it's starting to show. I wish she'd let me do more to help, though I know it's because Hadley doesn't know how much of her story I know. If I had known how bad it was, I would have dragged the woman out and made her stay with Kat or Ryan. I remember my mom being in a similar situation with her ex-boyfriend. Had she not had a nightmare that she was at her own viewing, I would have lost her. I remember my grandfather picked me up from school that day with no warning. Being a kid, only in third grade at the time, I was scared as hell when they picked me up in the middle of the day. It wasn't until they took me to my grandparents house, where my mom and I lived for several years after that, that they told me they moved us out while her ex was at work. My family was nervous the asshole would come for me if they didn't pick me up early.

"Bro, I'm glad you're finally getting some but goddamn, you're whipped." My friend laughs at his own joke.

"Kiss my ass, I'm worried about her. Her friend is in the hospital. Some shit went down and just - fuck," I huff out a breath, anger radiates through me at the memories of how my girl and Ryan were so broken when they found her. "They're not leaving Hadley's side."

I notice Johnny stiffen next to me; something shifts inside of him. He turns towards me with confusion and anger warring on his face. The bartender brings us another round, Johnny takes a long pull of the fresh Manhattan before he speaks.

"Hadley James?"

"Yea, her husband had been using her as a fucking punching bag for fuck knows how long and she tried to kill herself." I'm overwhelmed with rage as the moments of Kat and Ryan falling apart in my arms when Hadley was in surgery come flooding back again. "How do you know her?"

"I was good friends with her husband for a while. Hadley is special. She deserves a fuck ton better than that pussy," venom laces his voice. "Is she going to be ok?"

"They expect her to make a full recovery, physically at least." I take a swig of my Guinness, "mentally? Emotionally? We won't know until she wakes up."

Johnny grunts as he lifts his drink back to his lips. I can feel rage coming off him in waves. I know he was friends with Andy, but his reaction is a bit out of character. Usually, he's a sarcastic pain in my ass. He always has something to say, but before I can question him about the sudden shift in his behavior, my phone vibrates on the bar top.

Pickle:

> She woke up and kicked me out. At least for tonight, Ryan is staying, and I'll go back tomorrow.

Clay:

> That's great! I'm glad she's awake. How is she doing?

Pickle:

> She's broken. We'll get her through this though.

> Can I stay with you tonight? I don't want to be alone.

Clay:

> Princess, you don't need to ask; you can stay with me whenever you like.

Pickle:

> See you soon (kiss emoji)

I glance at Johnny who looks like he's ready to tear someone apart.

"Are you ok, Man?" I ask

"I will be," Johnny grunts in response.

"Bro, the fuck is going on?" I punch his shoulder to pull his attention.

"I should have known something was going on with him," he growls. The man actually growls at me. Ok, well not at me, but he growls his answer.

"The fuck?" Hiding my confusion is impossible.

"Nothing man, I'm good. Go get your girl. That's why you were grinning at your phone, right?" He smirks, but it doesn't quite reach his eyes though. Something is definitely going on here.

"You sure?" I arch a brow at him, questioning if I should actually leave him alone.

"Bro, get the fuck out of here. I'm good." He punches my shoulder, "tell Kat I said hi."

The drive back to my place feels like it takes twice as long. I climb the stairs from my office to reach my apartment. I take a deep breath as I let out a sigh of relief when I see her. She steps out of the bathroom, her body covered by a fluffy teal towel. I smirk to myself remembering she's the reason I bought that set. It's a near perfect match to her eyes and hair. I close the door behind me before removing the distance between us. I wrap myself around her small frame. I can't get close enough.

"Hey, Princess," is all I get out before she clings to me, and sobs tear through her. "Let it out, I'm here. I'm not going anywhere."

I lift her into my arms, carry her to my room, and lay her on the bed. I tug my shirt over my head and toss it over my shoulder. I hear a soft thud as it lands on the floor, before I crawl in beside her. She starts to shiver from the cool air hitting her still damp skin, so I pull the covers over us both to warm her. Dark circles under her eyes make the exhaustion even more apparent. She fights through the tears; in all of the time I've known her, she's only allowed herself to cry once in front of me. After she healed from her ex's departure from her life, she's refused to shed more than a few tears here and there.

"She could have died, we could have lost her because of him." She buries her face in my chest as she admits her fears, still not letting the dam fully break. My heart aches for her as she falls apart in my arms. For the three of them. They've become so close since they met not long after we opened the gym. She spiraled after her ex left, but that wasn't the first time she was abandoned.

"I know," I hold her against my chest, my hand cupping her head before I start to stroke her hair. She melts into me more with each stroke.

"It brought everything back, when we found her," she chokes out the words. "I saw Penny and Hadley simultaneously in that tub."

I hold her against me for a while, not speaking. There is nothing to say at this moment that can help her. It takes some time before her breathing steadies, telling me she's finally asleep. Not daring to release her, I settle in for the duration of the night. Taking her in, inhaling her scent, noticing the way she feels in my arms against my bare skin: she's perfection. From the moment I met her, even at her worst, she's always been perfect.

It clicks in that moment, maybe I shouldn't be so surprised by that. I haven't dated anyone since I met her. Sure, I've had a few one-night stands, but it's never been for anything more than a physical release. This sassy, incredible, frustrating and beautiful woman is my everything. I am unconditionally and irrevocably in love with her.

Fuck a duck. I did not just internally quote Bella Swan of all people. I groan inwardly at myself.

Chapter Thirteen

My eyes flutter open, my cheek is slick with sweat and drool after being buried in a bare broad muscular chest all night. I whimper as I inhale his scent. God this man has me unnerved from the moment I wake up just from his smell alone. Clay's arms tighten around me as soon as the sound passes my lips, making me giggle.

"Good morning, Princess." He leans down, burying his face into my neck. "Go back to sleep for a little while."

"Hi." I wrap myself around him holding him tight. "I can't. Ryan's been there all night and I still need to grab a change of clothes from my place. I feel terrible. I need to get back to them."

He grumbles into my neck, "not until after my breakfast."

"What?" I ask, needing clarification because with his gruff morning voice whatever he just said sounded like Cookie Monster after consuming an entire jar of cookies without milk.

A sly chuckle is my only warning before he flips me onto my back. The blankets no longer keep our cocoon of warmth intact. Another giggle escapes me as the cool air caresses my heated skin. Clay's mouth crashes against mine, teeth and tongues clashing together as we war for control of the kiss. When I finally relent, he deepens our connection. Hands roam and caress my bare skin, leaving goosebumps in their wake. I moan with every squeeze of my flesh in his strong hands.

"Clay," his name comes out as a plea. A plea for what? More? Less? I'm not sure.

"Princess, I need to taste you. It's been too long." His mischievous grin would melt my panties off if I still had any on. "Please."

"Yes," my response comes out nearly inaudible, a whisper that I'm shocked he hears.

Without a second thought or allowing any time to change my mind, Clay's face disappears down my body until his face is mere inches my cunt. I feel his breath against my skin and I tremble with anticipation. It really has been too long. I've missed him, his touch, everything about this man that drives me wild, yet brings me a solace I haven't known in so long.

"Fuck," is the last thing he says before his mouth covers my most private spot, his tongue delving between my folds and lapping up the arousal he's caused in such a short amount of time. I dig my nails into his scalp as his tongue flattens and applies the perfect pressure against my clit.

I scream out, the pleasure so overwhelming that my hips buck up against his face. His fingertips dig into my flesh, forcing me back down onto the mattress. I groan in frustration, which only makes him chuckle against my skin. The vibrations against my clit are overpowering, my toes curl almost painfully tight as I fly off the insurmountable cliff. My legs are shaky as the high of my release ebbs, but it's not enough.

"God, Clay, please!" I'm begging for more. The need for him to take me, to fill me is too much. "If you don't fuck me right now, I'll never forgive you." It comes out as a pathetic whimper, not the demand it's intended to be, but I don't care. I need this man like I need my next breath.

Clay sucks my clit into his mouth making me cry out in agony. He takes his time to climb up my body, peppering wet kisses coated in my arousal all along my skin. Once his lips reach mine, I pull him down to taste what's left of myself as I wrap my legs around his waist, digging my heels into his ass, urging him to take claim to the space between my thighs.

"Give me a second, Princess." His voice is light with amusement as he tries to pull away from me. "I need to get a condom."

"Clay, I'm on the pill. Don't make me wait." I groan as I thrust my hips up to meet him for some sort of friction.

I know the moment he understands my meaning. His beautiful eyes instantly darken as though someone flipped a switch. Clays lips crash against mine again as he notches himself at my entrance, not allowing any time to reconsider my decision before he slides his cock home. Filling me so perfectly I'm whimpering with need, I struggle against him in hopes that he will move, giving me what I want.

"Greedy, Princess." Clay groans against my lips before he gives into my desire. Slowly pulling back only to thrust back and fill me to the hilt once more.

"Oh god, Clay!" The lack of a barrier between us feels exquisite. My body humming with anticipation as he continues to fuck me. I dig my heels into his ass trying to pull him deeper each time he thrusts into me, not feeling close enough. He chuckles darkly as he moves to my neck, biting down hard as his hand finds its way between our bodies pinching my swollen bundle of nerves. I scream out when the best kind of agony rushes through my body. My toes curl and my back arches off the bed as I fall apart around his perfect cock.

"Fuck, Kat. Your pussy feels like it was made for me," Clay grunts out the words as his thrusts become erratic and he finally empties inside me with his release. He collapses on top of me, and we lay like that for a while before I remember that I have to leave to relieve Ryan.

"Text me later, ok, Princess?" His eyes are heavy with sleep, having worn himself out already this morning.

"As soon as I get to the hospital," I promise him, knowing I'll be at my place for a bit. The incredible sex was a distraction I needed, but I can feel the warring battle of sadness and memories inside me demanding to be set completely free.

I'm sitting on my bed, my emotions become unbearable as I sit still by myself for the first time since Hadley tried to end her life. As much as I need Clay, and as much as I've enjoyed the distraction that he provides me, there is only one person who is going to fully understand the pain I'm feeling. With trembling fingers, I find his number in my phone. Once I press the call button, I lift the phone to my ear. The line rings for less than a second before he answers.

"KitKat!" my big brother's voice is full of a joy he reserves for me.

"Auggie," I sob into the phone.

"Kat, what's wrong?" The easy-going demeanor immediately changes to one of concern and rage.

"It's...it's...she tried to. She tried to..." I can't get the words out.

"Don't move, we just finished a job an hour away." The call ends before my brain can form another word.

Time stops as I curl onto the bed and allow the pain, anxiety and turmoil from over the last week take hold. The tears start and don't stop. The 'what ifs' I've been trying to keep at the back of my mind force their way to the forefront. Sobs rack through my body, and I barely register when my bed dips until I feel a rough hand on my shoulder. I startle with a high-pitched scream that would rival Dean Winchester; I turn so quickly I nearly give myself whiplash.

"Auggie!? You're here?" I gasp when I see my big brother.

"My little sister calls me crying and unable to speak. I don't give a shit if gramps came back from the dead to have a chat, I'd drop anything for you." It's been years since I've seen him in person. He's always traveling for *work*.

"Auggie?" A tiny woman with her dark blonde hair in a loose braid repeats my nickname for my brother with a mischievous giggle. "Really?"

"Sunshine, don't even think about it, that is reserved for my sister." He growls, "I will not hesitate to take you over my knee."

"You already know it's happening." A second woman with the most stunning blue hair chimes on from behind the first girl.

"Ugh, fuck off." He groans with an adorable smile plastered on his face; he can't even pretend to be upset with them. What the.

"Who are they? Auggie?" My mind whirling at the intrusion, confused not knowing who these women are.

"Sorry sis, these are my girls, Echo, Chloe." His smile is so warm, "Ladies, this is my sister, Katrina." I don't miss his use of my government name.

"I love you, Auggie, but you can fuck off with Katrina. I will only answer to Kat." I snap at him, still clinging onto his chest.

"Aw! You're feisty, I like you." The blue haired girl grins at me. "I'm Chloe, this is Echo."

"It's nice to meet you both." I smile widely at them. It's the first time my brother has referred to anyone as his girl let alone two people. Shit, Hadley would lose her mind right now if she knew.

The thought of my best friend still stuck in the hospital has my tears falling once again. I hold onto my brother while I cry, the security that this man has provided me since I was born never fails to make me feel at ease.

"What happened, KitKat?" Auggie asks quietly.

I sniffle trying to control my breathing long enough to speak. "Hadley tried to kill herself and it took me back to Penny. I couldn't call her," I pause as my breathing becomes labored with anxiety again, "I just needed someone who would understand where my mind is. We were so close to losing her too."

His body goes as still as stone as what I've confessed becomes clear.

"You found her, didn't you?" His eyes filled with a pain he's avoided talking about for years. I just nod, no other words are needed. He understands, my mind has been in the past and present simultaneously over the last week as I've been at my best friend's bedside.

I just got home from a pool day with friends. We were celebrating my birthday and the last week of school. I've never been one for birthday parties, my preference has always been to celebrate those around me above myself. I rush into the house to find Auggie on the couch playing video games with a friend. I wave as I walk past them. Mom and Dad are still at work, even when they're here, they're working.

I cross the living room to the steps that lead to the second floor. Climbing the stairs two at a time, ready to wash the chlorine off my skin. I hear running water as I approach the bathroom our sister Penny and I share.

"Ugh! Pen! I need a shower, how long are you gonna be?" I call through the closed bathroom door. She doesn't answer, so I push the bathroom door open only to find her nearly fully submerged in red tinged water. "AH-HHHHHHHHHHHHHHHH." The scream that leaves my chest could rival that of Jamie Lee Curtis, the scream queen herself.

Auggie and his friend come barreling up the stairs to find us. Our brother leaps over me and drags Penny's limp body from the water. She's still fully clothed in an oversized t-shirt and sweatpants, which she's made her entire personality recently. Auggie wraps mom's white towels around her wrists. Meanwhile his friend Ron pulls me to the side, as he grabs his flip phone from his pants pocket. Time goes still for me as we wait for the ambulance to arrive at our house. The medics revive our sister and Auggie and I go with her in the ambulance. They still haven't been able to get ahold of our parents. It's no surprise.

Months, it takes months before Penny is released to come home. She is held at a facility that will only allow us to see her if our parents are with us. Spoiler alert, they never are. The nurses grow tired of me quickly; calling multiple times a day to check on her and to be able to hear her voice. I need to know she didn't leave me while I couldn't see her.

I shake my head in an attempt to clear the unwanted memories from my mind. It's been so long since I've recalled that day. Since I've allowed myself to relive those moments from a past that holds so many awful memories. Finding Hadley brought so much back I've long since forced myself to forget. I look up at my big brother who looks so broken and lost in the same past.

"I didn't mean to pull you away from anything Auggie, I just needed to hear your voice. It's been so long, and you know she won't talk about this." I sigh.

"Don't you dare apologize, I promised you both when you need me, I'm here." His face is serious. "Is Hadley going to be, ok?"

"She woke up yesterday. She made me go home for the night and then trade off with Ry tonight. I just got back to change and it's the first time I've been alone, and I just lost myself." I admit.

"You just got back?" He cocks an accusatory brow at me.

"Oh," I giggle. "You know Clay?"

"It's about fucking time." I hear Chloe call from the doorway, my cheeks flush.

Just how long has he been with them?

"Chloe!" Echo hisses next to her, wrapping her arms around the taller girl's middle.

"Sorry, she has no filter," Auggie chuckles, "and she's been rooting for the two of you since I told them I thought you liked Clay and were being too much of a pussy to make a move."

"Hey!" I can't help but laugh. My mind lost somewhere between the past and present, horrid memories fighting with a comical situation that is creating new ones. "I like you." I repeat Chloe's earlier words back to her.

"Are you going to be ok, Kat?" he asks as he pulls away from me, staring down at me.

"I will be. I just wish I could talk to her without them getting involved," I groan. Bile rises in my stomach at the thought of our parents. I'm so not ready to relive that right now.

"You call me if anything else happens, yea?" He squeezes me to his chest.

"Always." I promise.

After a quick visit and my attempt to distract myself by getting to know Chloe and Echo, they inform me they need to leave. Another job is scheduled in a few days, and they need to start the trip immediately. I know it wasn't much, but even being able to see him for a short time like this gives me strength. I know he's not necessarily into the most legal of careers, but he's doing it for Penny and the trauma she's endured. Even if she refuses to fully disclose what that trauma is to me.

I follow them outside, locking the door behind me.

"Hey, wait. My door was locked. How did you get in?" I ask over my shoulder.

Echo giggles and winks at me as she disappears into a dark sedan. I shake my head, laughing at the ridiculousness. They are kind of perfect for him.

Chapter Fourteen

S tunning red hair flutters in the breeze, catching my attention as I walk from my car to the entrance of the hospital. A beautiful woman with the reddest hair I've ever seen stands at the door waiting. It's even brighter than Kayleigh's, which says a lot. Something seems familiar about her that I can't quite figure out as I approach.

"Kat?" The woman who I must have met somewhere greets me. "Are you Kat?"

I hear a slight accent, and it clicks. Alannah.

"What are you doing here? I can't let you up to see her." I rush out.

"I'm not here to see her, you haven't responded to me, and I figured this was going to be the easiest way to contact you." She sighs. "Am I crazy for tracking you down like this? Probably, but my big brother has done more for me than anyone else in my life. I'm going to do what I can for him. I just need something, anything."

I shake my head, if it were anyone else, I would be skeptical of her sincerity. My eyes dart around the entryway, knowing Ryan is likely on her way down here.

"Listen, Ry will kick my ass if she knows I'm talking to you." Guilt consumes me, but more so that the lack of information has caused Connor pain when he's brought so much joy to our friend. "We made a deal not to tell him anything without her permission. Can we meet for a drink tomorrow around this time when Ry and I switch off again?"

"Where?"

"Finley's?" The name slips out, out of habit.

"Thank you." She smiles sweetly at me before she walks past me and vanishes between cars in the parking lot.

"Where the hell have you been?" Ryan's face is light and ready to cause trouble.

"Uhm," I giggle. "I stayed the night with Clay."

"Uh huh, and..." She taunts, looking for the tea. "Go on."

"Ry, leave her be." Hadley chimes in from the bed next to her. "If she wants to tell you about his dick she will."

That last part, she was absolutely teasing and needling me to spill it.

"Ok, fine!" I whine.

"Yes!" They cheer in unison.

Before I can go into detail, her nurse and transport aid come in to take Hadley for imaging. *Saved by the damn MRI.*

"Really, where have you been?" Her tone is now serious. "Clay texted me because you haven't responded to him and left hours ago."

"I went home and cried, I called Auggie, and he was close, so they came to check on me." I smile at the memory.

"They?" She asks, confused because she knows he has been alone since the day he left.

"He found these two women. They're all together." I whisper, not wanting Hadley to hear after Andy. Ryan, out of all people, would be the least likely to judge, considering she's bi. Hell, we used to sleep together. "They're kind of perfect for him."

"Well, shit." Her gentle smile gives me hope. "You may want to let Clay know; he was starting to freak out."

"Thanks, babes." I wrap my arms around her tiny frame and hold her. My face buried in her neck as I regained my composure. When I pull away, she leaves her hands on my hips. Her eyes sear into mine.

"Have you talked to Penny?" Her question comes out as a whisper.

Tears prick at my eyes at her question. I shake my head, unable to speak.

"Have you tried?" The prodding today is frustrating.

"She won't talk about it. Even if I call her, she still lives with them. I don't want them involved in my life, I can't." My voice goes up a few octaves. I get so mad whenever the dreaded subject of my parents comes up, even in passing.

"Breathe, baby girl. I'm not going to force anything. I was just asking." She squeezes me tight again. "When she is doing better, I think you should tell Hadley about your sister."

I shake my head violently at the suggestion. "Absolutely not, that would devastate her and cause even more trauma. Absolutely not."

"Just think about it, ok?" Ryan releases me from her hold. "Keep me posted when you find out the results. I am going to shower and sleep for a week. I'll see you tomorrow," she jokes before strolling out of the room.

I pull out my phone to see multiple calls and even more texts from Clay.

Crap.

Kat:

I'm so sorry, it was the first time I allowed myself to feel my feelings and broke down. I called Auggie and he came by before they passed through town. I'm with Hadley now.

Clay:

Thank fuck you're ok, Princess! I was just worried. I'm glad you are with her.

Kat:

I am, I'm so sorry for not responding sooner.

A soft knock at the door pulls my attention from the phone. I glance up to see Clay standing in the doorway. An easy smile takes over my face when I see him. I stand to my feet, but before I can walk to him, he crosses the room in two long strides with his long freaking legs.

"What are you doing here?" I ask as I loop my arms around his neck.

"Princess, I was on my way here before you responded. I stopped by your house, and when I didn't see your car, I panicked since Ryan hadn't heard from you either." He presses his face into my hair as he inhales my scent.

"I feel awful." I admit, "I didn't mean to worry you." I pull him down onto the couch across from the hospital bed and explain what happened. From falling asleep to Auggie showing up, which surprised the hell out of me.

"Baby, I'm not upset with you. I was just worried." His arms are wrapped so tightly around me as he croons the words against my ear.

"I don't know what I'd do without you," I admit.

"You'll never have to find out. You're stuck with me, Kat." I feel his smile against my ear.

I close my eyes, just savoring the closeness. As I'm melting into him, I hear voices bringing me back to reality. Hadley is being wheeled back into the room and smiles brightly when she sees us together. "So, you couldn't wait to dick her down again until tomorrow?" She chuckles wildly at her own joke.

"Oh my god, you have spent too much time with Ryan!" I can feel my face redden as my skin flames.

Clay is just quietly laughing next to me. "Hey, Had."

"You two don't need to stay." I hear the sadness in her voice that she's been trying so hard to hide. "Really. Go home with him, Kat. I'll be ok."

"Not a chance babe. You're not being left alone. I will climb in that bed and snuggle you to sleep if you try to fight me on it." I waggle my eyebrows at her.

She chuckles while shaking her head at me. Hadley and I have never crossed that line in our friendship. She's never been interested in women, but she does encourage my equal opportunity snuggles when given a chance.

"It's alright, I'm not staying, you two can cuddle. I just needed to see my girl and make sure she's ok." He pulls away, pinching my chin between his thumb and forefinger as he lifts my face to press the softest kiss against my lips. I whimper at the chaste connection. "I'll see you tomorrow."

He winks at me before turning to Hadley who has climbed back into her bed. He walks to her and presses a soft kiss to her forehead before he says something so quiet against her hair that I can't hear him.

"Goodnight, Clay." Hadley smiles at him like he hung the moon as he walks out of the room.

I wonder what that was all about.

Chapter Fifteen

We're both a bundle of anxiety waiting on the test results from the MRI earlier. The night drags on until we receive the news from the doctors. They find no indication of what could become permanent damage and she's healing better than expected at an accelerated rate. They're sending her to the inpatient psychiatric wing for at least a week to make sure she's ok with what caused this attempt and give her some better coping strategies. Amy, the therapist who will be rounding in the hospital this week, has taken her on. She's been in the room with us for the last twenty minutes, going over the initial intake information. I tried to leave, but Hadley insisted I stay because she doesn't want to hide anything from Ryan or myself anymore.

"So, the plan is, over the next week we will spend quite a bit of time together." Amy explains. "Our goal is to get down to what caused your current state and how we can get you to move forward in a healthier manner."

"Ok," Hadley quietly agrees. "I don't want to have to be drugged for the rest of my life."

"Well, I can't guarantee anything at this point." Amy goes into sensitive therapist mode, which is kind of wild to watch from an outside perspective. "In my opinion, it would be beneficial for you to continue what has been prescribed while you've been here. I can decide if we can reduce or eliminate anything as we work together. But we need to let your body and your mind rest a little bit and the medication will help you do that."

Hadley doesn't respond verbally this time, just a quick nod as tears stream down her cheeks. Ryan strolls in, just in time to see Hadley's tears and Amy sitting at her bedside.

"Who are you? What happened?" She races in, wrapping herself around Hadley protectively.

"Hi Ryan, I'm Amy." Amy chuckles, instinctively knowing who the woman is that has gone into momma bear mode with our friend.

Ryan relaxes recognizing the name since we had been texting about the therapist earlier in the day.

"Oh, hi!" Ryan's cheeks tinge pink, "Sorry, I thought something bad happened."

Amy says her goodbyes and tells Hadley she'll see her for their first session tomorrow and that we won't be able to stay the night with her while she is in the psychiatric wing. Ryan's eyes immediately find mine; apprehension mirrored in one another's gaze. My smart watch vibrates, telling me it's time to leave to meet Alannah, which is the worst timing after that revelation, but I know she will absolutely march her behind up here if I don't meet her.

"I have to run out for a bit, but I'll come back and spend the night with you both in a little while." I announce to my friends.

"Get out of here, go have fun with Clay. Ry can let you know when visiting hours for the loony bin are." Hadley jokes.

"No, I want to-," I don't even get to finish my sentence before Hadley tosses a pillow at me.

"I'm not standing in the way of you getting the D, Pickle." She's all smiles as she waves a hand, shooing me.

I don't have time to feign offense because the moment I go for a sarcastic and dramatic response my phone vibrates in my hand.

Alannah:

I'll be there in ten minutes.

Shit.

Kat:

I'm leaving now.

Alannah:

I'll get us a table.

I walk into Finley's, the song Good Lookin' by Dixon Dallas streams loudly through the speakers. I giggle as the lyrics 'He's bouncing off my booty cheeks' sound as soon as I spot Alannah who is sitting alone at a back corner table. Her long red hair is styled in loose waves that cascade down across her chest. I cross the room and slide into the chair across from her.

"Howya," her smile is warm and welcoming.

"Hi," I return the smile.

Our server, a young woman with blonde hair wrapped in space buns on top of her head, strides over with a customer service smile splitting her face.

"Hi, ladies. I'm Haley and I'll be your server today. What can I get for you?" She asks politely enough.

My smile fades when she introduces herself. Her name being so close to my friend.

"I'll take an espresso martini." Alannah responds.

"Mm, that sounds good, I'll take one too. Thanks, Haley." I smile weakly at her before turning back to Alannah.

"I know he's been in contact with you. You know about Andy?" She's getting straight to the point. I like it.

"Yes, he told us. We haven't mentioned it to her. She's still healing." I take a deep breath as Haley returns and hands us our drinks. I take a long pull before I continue. "She was in a medically induced coma for a few days until the injuries were under control enough for her to be safely pulled out of it."

"Shite," I notice her Irish accent is thicker with some words more than others. It's adorable. "Yes. As far as what all transpired," I drink a little more of the martini, "I can't tell you that part of her story."

"She's awake now?" It's clear she's concerned. "Is she going to be, ok?"

"Yes," I breathe. "I don't know how long it's going to take for her to be back to one hundred percent, but she will get there."

"Alright." She nods, "Connor has been beside himself. He doesn't know any of this, just that she's been in the hospital since the same day that Andy attacked him."

"We didn't feel right telling him anything more than that." I admit, "there is so much more to what happened, she's not ready and we don't feel right putting more on his plate."

"That's stupid. He could be there for her." Alannah huffs, disgusted with the reasoning I share with her.

I take a few moments to piece together what I can tell her. Ryan and I may seem selfish for our decision to keep him out of it because they are so annoyingly in love, but I don't regret it.

"It may be, but she hasn't asked for him. She's not ready to see him." I sigh, "When she is ready to tell him, she will. You've seen them together, right? Their love is nauseating. She's not going to give him up without a real fight. This is her way of fighting. Give it time."

Alannah chuckles under her breath, "It is a bit over the top, but in a beautiful way. I used to have that with my husband, once upon a time." Her face falls, "I'd give anything to have that again." She admits.

"I didn't think I'd have it again after my ex-girlfriend left me." My heart aches for her, I only know some of her story, "I think I've found it again with my boyfriend, Clay."

She nods in response; a weak smile tugs at her lips.

"Don't give up. I only know that your husband is," I pause unsure how to broach the subject, "no longer with us."

"You can say it," she lets out a dark laugh. "He was killed. It's been a long time. It still hurts but the fact is, he's dead."

"Well, that got dark fast," I stare at her blankly before we both laugh. "My point is you will find someone. Put yourself out there, I may have been friends with Clay for years beforehand, but who knows who you'll find."

We continue to chat for a while, sharing some fried pickles, which she thoroughly enjoys too. The girls constantly tease me, but I can't help my love of pickles. Especially the Wickles Dirty Dills. There is something so heavenly about them that I could eat them every day. Yea, I know. It's weird, don't judge me.

A few hours and several drinks later, I feel like I know Alannah almost as well as I do Ry and Hadley. It's weird. We clicked so easily. It was easy with my girls but with Alannah, it was almost like my soul clicked into place. A platonic soulmate, maybe.

Chapter Sixteen

Sleep has never felt so good, and my dreams never feel this vivid. Her lips press the softest kisses against my bare chest. Long teal waves curtain either side of her face, hiding her impeccable features as she trails down my middle. A soft nip and suck here and there and my cock is standing at full attention. I'm so hard, I can feel the blood as it pumps through my engorged length.

Her delicate hands set in place on my stomach while her head bobs up and down my cock. The way her bright eyes shine in the streaks of moonlight from the window have my balls tightening, I haven't been with her enough. My fingers wrap around her soft strands. And as much as I enjoy the feel of her mouth, I need more of her. All of her. I gently coax her to release my dick which she does with an audible pop that has my cock ready to burst.

Oh my god. This isn't a dream.

Soft supple thighs are gripping my hips as my cock disappears inside of her perfectly pink pussy. My eyes shoot open at the sensation of her cunt squeezing my cock as she rides my length. *Jesus Christ.*

"Oh, my fucking god." I groan as the sleep flits from my eyelids, "Princess!"

The slow pace that she's set has me on edge. It's an incredible yet cruel feeling. I grip her hips, my nails bite into the soft flesh. An almost inaudible moan escapes her as she continues her sensual assault.

"Princess," I thrust up inside her, a loud cry sounds from her as I fill her even deeper from below. "I am not going to last," I admit.

"Please, Clay. I'm not ready for this to end." She begs, and she does it so beautifully I can't deny her.

Fuck.

I filter images through my mind of everything from Mickey Mouse on Ice to House of a Thousand Corpses because no way in hell can I get off with that image in my mind. I squeeze her hips, the silent plea not to move anymore so I can catch my breath. A devious glint shines in her eyes as she intentionally squeezes my cock with her annoyingly magical cunt.

"Kat!" I roar and flip us so that she lands on her back in one swift motion. My hips slam into her as I bury myself.

"I." *Thrust.* "Will." *Thrust.* "Make." *Thrust.* "You." *Thrust.* "Pay." *Thrust.* "For." *Thrust.* "That." *Thrust.* I pant each word.

No matter how much I try to ignore the sensation of being bare inside her, it's too much. I slide my hand between us and rub tight circles around her clit for a few moments before I feel my balls tighten and the base of my spine tingle. I jut my hips forward, pinching her swollen clit between my fingers. Her climax is instant and explosive. Her walls ripple around me, forcing my cock free as I reach my own completion. Spurts of my pearly white release land on her puffy lips, the proof of her late-night use of my body displayed on her soft skin.

"Jesus, that was so much better than I expected." Kat pants after I collapse on top of her. My chest heaves as I try to catch my own breath. She starts another thought but then stops to try to figure out how to end the sentence, "that was..."

"That was something I'm going to need you to repeat, and often." I lift my head and press a soft kiss against her lips.

She giggles, which doesn't do anything to help my dick which is already growing again at the vibration of her laughter.

"I thought you were going to stay at the hospital after your dinner?" I ask as I roll onto my side, pulling her with me.

"Hadley insisted that I spend the night with you. I'm not sure what you said to her to make her so insistent." She tries her best to level me with a glare.

"Princess, you're adorable." I tease, "I just told her that you and Ryan need her just as much as she needs you two."

Kat is quiet for a few minutes and then rolls me back onto my back, pressing her lips to mine, coaxing me with her sweet tantalizing tongue for entry. I groan allowing her access and we get lost in one another again.

Johnny has finished his last burpee when his gaze meets mine. I'm on my third coffee of the day. The fuck fest last night was incredible but goddamn, I don't even know the last time I spent that many hours going at it with someone. My cock twitches in my shorts. I've never been so thankful to have on bike shorts underneath.

"You look rough." His tone is light, but his eyes are sad. "Late night?"

"Kiss my ass." I throw his towel at him.

He chuckles darkly knowing exactly what happened without the words needing to be said. It's not until he tosses the towel back at me that he relaxes. He lets out a long steady breath before he speaks again.

"I'm going to be moving back home soon." His eyes flicker away from my face. "My grandfather isn't doing well and when he's gone my mother will need help taking over the family business."

"I'm so sorry man, that's rough." I clap a hand onto his shoulder. "Do you need anything?"

He shakes his head no.

"When are you leaving?" I ask.

"I'm still waiting for a date from my mom. She doesn't want me there, at least not until my presence is necessary." His laugh is harsh and unlike the easy-going man I've known these past few years. "My family is... unique."

"I'd say." I furrow my brow at his odd response.

"Well, let's make the most of what time we have left." I chuckle as I continue, "Besides, it's not like we'll never see each other again. We're not kids, bro. We can travel without asking our parents for permission." I chuckle at my own joke.

The next thirty minutes of our session goes by at a snail's pace. I'm not sure if it's the fact that I now know one of my best friends is moving or if it's because no matter how much coffee I get into my system I can't evade the exhaustion from last night's escapades. It's really anyone's guess at this point.

Chapter Seventeen

My muscles are so tight as my brain and body find its way back to consciousness. I stretch in an attempt to wake my sore limbs from the night filled with immense pleasure. I've never felt so emboldened to wake a partner like that, both giving and taking pleasure at the same time before they were even aware of what was happening. It was so freaking hot; I can't imagine anything better.

My back is cooler than it should be, Clay was wrapped too tight around me to be this cold. I reach behind me to find an empty spot where my man should be. I roll over just to confirm he's not here. I whine and flop back onto my pillow. My phone vibrates with a notification.

Clay:

> Princess, enjoy a day off. When you wake up go spend time with Ryan and Hadley.

> Don't argue with me, I'll take you over my knee. Actually, go ahead and argue, I'd like to turn your ass red.

I giggle to myself before I type a response.

Kat:

> This is me arguing with you, from your bed.

I attach a sexy selfie right after the text goes through. My chest is barely covered by the sheet. My stomach is bare, and my leg is peeking out, my pussy is just barely covered.

Clay:

> Princess, getting me hard while I am working with Leigh is the cruelest kind of torture.

I do a double take reading his message, a wild laugh erupts from my chest. Should I feel bad about the boner I just caused with him being in such close proximity to looney Leigh? Probably, I totally don't though. My giggles continue as I throw the sheets off and climb out of bed. I wiggle my toes into the soft plush carpet, it feels oddly satisfying being that I'm so used to the hardwood floors at my place.

Several moments of stretching later, my limbs are ready to move. When I reach the bathroom there is a fresh towel and a note.

> *Princess,*
>
> *I hope you slept well, come find me when you wake up. If I'm with Leigh, make up any reason to pull me away. Hell, make up any reason to pull me away no matter who I'm with.*
>
> *See you soon, gorgeous.*
>
> *P.S. I'm jealous of this towel.*

A serene smile pulls at the corners of my mouth as I turn on the shower. It only takes a few seconds for the water to heat up. I step into the large shower. It really is spacious, we could both fit in here, comfortably. The hot water streams down the length of my body, my skin tingles red, not just from the heat but from the memories of last night. Never in my life have I felt comfortable enough to initiate anything with a man, even a kiss. It was always them making the first move. The level of solace this incredible man gives me just by existing in my presence is staggering.

My bright pink loofah and wild cherry blossom body wash call to me. I squeeze out a generous amount of the body wash, lather up the loofa and scrub my skin. I immediately feel refreshed when the unique fragrance reaches my senses. Suds of lathered up soap slowly drip down my body. Feeling a bit emboldened, I snag my phone from where I left it within reach, outside of the shower, and I snap a few selfies. My face isn't in them, but he'll obviously know it's me. I draft a quick message.

Kat:

Are you only jealous of the towel? (Sudsy selfie attached)

Clay:

You are playing with fire, beautiful. (smirking devil emoji)

Feeling quite proud of myself, I rinse my body and step out of the shower. With the towel wrapped tightly around my chest so nothing is visible. I walk out of the bathroom and make my way to the bedroom. I let out a frustrated sigh when I realized I have no spare clothes. Several moments of digging through Clay's drawers later I find a pair of his gym shorts and a baggy T-shirt. Not the one I want, but I'll get to claim that one eventually.

Clay is leaning against a machine talking to a client when I finally make my appearance in Karma. My cheeks tingle the brightest tint of red when I see him. I've never felt so hot in my own skin before. A devilish smirk splits his face, he excuses himself from his client and closes the distance between us in only a few long strides. His fingers tangle around mine and he pulls me back toward the office. Once inside, he closes the door, so we are secluded from everyone else currently present.

No words have a chance to pass between us as he pushes me against the solid door. His strong hand grips my throat as he pins me in place. His hard, sweat drenched body is pressed flush against my freshly bathed one. His mouth crashes against mine in a feverous kiss that seems to last forever. But it might only be for a few seconds, my body is too overstimulated to be able to understand the concept of time.

I breathe into him as the kiss continues, he lifts me up, holding my ass in his hands firmly. My legs wrap snugly around his waist, his hard length pressed so firmly against my clit my eyes roll back. Soft whimpers echo around the small space. His hands find the hem of the shirt that I'm wearing, I feel his fingers lightly grazing my middle before sliding up to my bare chest. Of course I chose to not wear a bra today. I'm not supposed to be peopling right now. But, goddamn, do I love to people with him. His hand cups my breast and his fingers fumble around in the heated moment before he tightly pinches my nipple. I cry out at the incredible sensation, a mixture of pleasure and pain. It's almost too much. Almost.

"Princess," he pants as he pulls his lips away from mine for a second and then his lips are back on my jaw, pressing a trail of wet, delicious kisses down the column of my throat. "Do you think you deserve to feel that release I know you so badly need right now, after being so dirty while I was stuck down here?" He grinds his hips against my center, and his rock-hard length presses against me again in just the right spot.

"Please," I whimper so desperately it's almost pathetic. No, it is pathetic, but the way this man can work my body like his own personal instrument is worth the embarrassment. "Please, Clay." I plead again for good measure.

He releases me back to my feet, my breath coming out in pants. I glare up at him expecting him to just let me walk around with a blue bean all day. Ok, I mean it's fair, I did tease him. Fuck. I totally deserve it. Equal opportunity teasing. I get it. Karma – rude.

In one swift motion, the shorts I had put on upstairs are around my ankles. So thankful that I have no panties on when I hear the appreciative growl come from my man.

"Turn around. Bend over." He barks out the order in one quick breath.

Oh god, why is this so hot!

I do as he says, knowing if he's going to take me, he's going to make sure I find my own release. I place my hands on the edge of the desk, my nails biting into the wood, ready for whatever he's going to give me. A quick swish of the air behind me is the only warning I have before a harsh sting erupts on my ass cheek. A second later the same thing happens on the other side. I yelp quietly at each point of contact.

"Clay," I plead.

"Beautiful, this is going to be rough and fast. Hold the fuck on." His voice is husky dripping with arousal.

"Fuck me." I barely recognize my own voice as I beg him to take me.

My already sore pussy from the hours of pounding he supplied last night takes him with only some protest, considering I've been in a constant state of arousal since the first time he ate my pussy on his kitchen counter. - As soon as he's fully rooted inside me, my walls contract around his generous size. He knows what he's doing, I'll give him that.

He takes what he wants from me, his hips slam against my ass as he pumps violently into me. I whimper at the sensation and the sound of our bodies connecting. After a few seconds he pulls out and I let out a breathy cry as soon as I feel the emptiness.

"Clay! Please!" I beg him again. A dark low throaty laugh leaves him before he fills me again. "Fuuuucccckkkk me." I mewl.

He continues at this rate for what feels like forever. My clit is throbbing it hurts so bad, I'm pretty sure if a soft breeze blew across my pussy right now, I'd explode. After the fifth or sixth time of this delicious torture I speak up.

"Please, let me come." I beg him. "Please, Clay."

He bends himself in half, his lips press against the sensitive skin on my neck just below my jaw. One hand is resting on my spine as the other wraps around my front, pinching a nipple between his fingers. I gasp at the pleasure the bit of pain elicits. "Yea, I think you've earned it now, Beautiful." He whispers against my skin as his hand disappears between my thighs and firmly presses against the sensitive bud. His thick cock is pumping inside of me yet again, but this time, he doesn't stop. He applies more pressure to my clit with each thrust until I feel him pulsing inside of my tight pussy. He lets out a string of curses as he finds his release at the same time that I detonate around him. My pussy ripples around his girthy cock, the need only partially sated. Clay's hips stutter as he fills me with his seed. He doubles over as he pants, playfully laying his weight onto my back.

"Please, tease me like that as often as you like if I get to punish you like that every time." I feel the grin against my skin before I force us both to a standing position.

"I need to go shower again" I whine, Clay spins me to face him and pulls me into his arms his mood is still light.

"No, I want you to feel me dripping down your thighs all day and I want you to smell like me while you're out doing whatever you are doing." He grins.

We have Hadley back a week later. While I miss falling asleep with Clay every night, I know my friend needs me more right now. My own needs can wait for now, I need to make sure she's ok. I can't risk losing her. Hadley and Ryan are cuddling on Ryan's large couch while I'm standing here in the kitchen making popcorn for a movie night. Why on earth they decided to watch Starship Troopers is beyond me.

I pull the bag out of the microwave and grab down a bowl to pour the popcorn into a bowl for easier access than the bag. If I'm going to be stuck watching this movie and not with my man, I'm going to at least stuff my face with something salty. Ok, maybe I'm a little frustrated, but I would never complain to them. I don't want Hadley to feel any worse than she already does.

My phone vibrates on the counter with a notification.

Penny:

Hey, Sis.

Chapter Eighteen

I've been staring at this text sporadically throughout the day. Let's be real here, I've been staring every single day since it came through a week ago. I haven't found the nerve to respond and if I'm honest, I'm terrified of what she's going to say. What they're going to have to say. The last time I heard from my sister was when my ex-girlfriend dumped me. When my heart was broken into a million pieces, they decided it was the perfect time to strike. Our parents pushed her to find out if I had learned my lesson, or if I still planned to live in sin like the whore I've always been. *Yea, you read that right.*

It was a blast; my heart was just broken and then my family forced her to break it all over again. Should I be mad at her? Probably, but since she tried to take her own life, she's been different. There have been so many times she dissociates and ends up in a catatonic state. It's not safe for her to be on her own so she's forced to do their bidding. It's that or they've threatened many times to have her admitted into a group home. Due to the nature of her mental health and inability to be by herself, they've got her locked into a guardianship.

Her doctors say it's from her traumatic events which caused her to act out and try to take her life. I wish I knew what exactly those experiences were, maybe I could help. If only she would allow me to be there for her, to shoulder some of the burden of whatever happened to her. According to what I've been told, until she is ready to face the trauma, she will likely not be able to work her way past these issues or be able to be on her own.

Steam surrounds me where I sit on the toilet, the fluffy purple cover of the lid keeps my bare legs from freezing on the porcelain in Ryan's bathroom. I have a large white towel wrapped around my naked body. I love how she has her entire place decorated. Photos she's taken cover every single wall. Whether it be in frames like here in the bathroom or canvas everywhere else in her space. She loves to be surrounded by those she loves and what she loves. The shower is still running even though I got in, washed up and got out all within a few minutes. I've still left the water on for at least twenty minutes. I don't want Ryan or Hadley to come looking for me. They'll most likely think I'm playing with myself, wouldn't be the first time any of us have gotten off in the shower while the others were hanging out in the other room. *What can I say, we're open about our sex lives, at least with each other.*

My chest heaves as I take a deep breath. I'm not ready for this but I need to do it. I tap the phone screen and type out the message before hitting send. Three strikes to the screen and that's it, it's sent.

Kat:

The response comes quickly. It must be a good day for her.

Penny:

Sis! I've missed you! How are you?

Kat:

I miss you. Is everything ok?

I ignore her question and ask my own. I'm not ready to share any specifics until I know the real reason behind this sudden contact.

Penny:

I'm good! It's been so long, I just wanted to check on you. After everything, I mean.

Kat:

After everything?

Penny:

uhmmm...

Kat:

Pen, what do you mean, after everything?

Penny:

Auggie may have called me to see if I had heard from you.

That son of a bitch! He knew I didn't want to involve her.

> Don't be mad at him. I understand why you didn't want to talk to me. Nothing I will ever do or say can make up for what happened last time we talked. I promise, I'm not reaching out for them. I've been doing better. Auggie has been forcing me to talk more about it.

> I'm glad you're doing better but I will stay mad at him. He had no right. This wasn't his place.

I open another message thread to text my brother.

> Augustus Kensington, the next time I see you, I will take you down like I used to when we were kids. I don't care how much bigger you are than me.

> Goodie, Pen finally messaged you. How long did it take you to respond?

> Have I mentioned I hate you?

> Love you too, sis!

While I know he meant well by telling Penny what happened, it pisses me off that he reached out to her when I told him I didn't want to. What's worse is the fact that he knows I didn't respond to her the moment the message came through. Asshole.

[text]

Penny:

> I just want to make sure you're ok. I know how hard it was on you when I...

I don't respond, there is nothing more for me to say. I make quick work of getting dressed in an oversized T-shirt and a pair of blue cotton boy shorts. There is no need for pants, it's just the three of us.

My mind is flooded with so many emotions as I return to the living room where Ryan and Hadley are sitting with their E-readers. It's quiet as I approach until Ryan notices me and she looks up with a teasing smirk on her face.

"Nice stems," she giggles.

"Oh! Can we watch that tonight?" Hadley chimes in excitedly, her eyes still on whatever she's reading.

I shake my head with a laugh. Of course, those two words would have us getting lost in the world with Cher and Dionne tonight. Though, a young Paul Rudd isn't a bad time. Who am I kidding? That man has aged like a fine wine, he will never, not be a beautiful specimen.

"Only if there is coffee, I need an extra jolt." I negotiate as if it's not a given that we'll be watching it even if there were a remote possibility they'd say no.

Five minutes later, we're all cuddled up on the couch under a blanket with coffee in hand and watching the cult classic, Clueless.

Chapter Nineteen

One Month Later

This past month has been a whirlwind of crazy. Hadley and the girls have been bouncing back and forth between Ryan's place and Kat's, so I only see her at work. We may take some time for a repeat of the quickie in the office everyday but it's not nearly enough. My sheets no longer smell like her, I've even worn her favorite band T-shirt a few times at the gym to tempt her to follow me upstairs and take it off just so I can get her in my bed again. Not necessarily for sex, although, I wouldn't say no. She's a firecracker between the sheets, well, and in the shower, my office, the kitchen, on the couch...you get the picture.

She's been working with clients all day today and hasn't had a break for our usual office rendezvous. My cock has been hard all damn day as I watch her. The way her tight shorts show off her curvaceous ass should be illegal. I've caught her eyes on me several times throughout the day, like she's purposefully teasing me. This woman will be the death of me, and oh my, what a death it will be.

The clock strikes eight o'clock and it's closing time. Kat is saying goodbye to her last client of the day and turns back toward the office. I notice a sexy saunter about her as she walks away from me while I lock up. *What did I ever do to deserve such torture?*

I expect to find her in the office waiting for me, but instead of seeing her perched on top of my desk, the door leading up to my apartment is open. I run up the steps to find her, closing the door behind me. She's nowhere in sight when I reach the top of the stairs.

"Kat?" I call out for her, still no response.

What the fuck. When I don't find her in the bathroom, I traipse back toward my room. The sight in front of me is one I will never grow tired of. Kat is laying on my bed in the shirt, you know the one. Just the shirt. She has a wide smile on her face, she knows she has me for whatever the hell she wants. I lean against the doorframe waiting for her to say whatever is on her mind before I wrap myself up in her for as long as I can.

"Soooooo..." Kat draws out the word, "Did I mention that we moved Hadley into her new apartment yesterday?"

"You didn't," I reply.

She has a mischievous twinkle in her eye, "Did I also forget to mention that she wanted to be on her own tonight?"

"It seems that it slipped your mind, Princess." My lips turn up into a grin as I push off the doorframe and close the distance between us, ready to get lost in what's *mine*. My hands find her ankles and yank her to the edge of the bed before I drop to my knees in front of her. Her scent envelopes me before I have the shirt pulled up to expose her. Kat's legs fall open dragging the shirt up her thighs to reveal she's completely bare under my shirt. "Princess." I growl as the blood pumping through my veins grows hot with anticipation. "You smell like my favorite meal come to life." I chuckle darkly before I dip my face down to meet her sensitive skin.

Her breath hitches as I nip gently at the spot just above her clit. An eager cry passes Kat's lips as she digs her nails into the sheets trying to find something for purchase as I make a show of just how slow and torturous I can be. My tongue swipes the length of each lip before my mouth presses a wet kiss to each thigh. Her legs begin to tremble with each wicked swipe of my tongue. It only takes a few moments before she cries out with a plea on her lips, begging me to allow her release.

"Princess, you've been tormenting me all day, don't you think I should get to return the favor?" I grin up at her from between her legs.

"Fuck!" Kat's whimper echoes throughout the room.

"In due time, beautiful, in due time." I taunt.

A rush of wind swirls around me as I walk inside The Mud House a few days later. I know Kat has a thing for the Mocha Mud Puddle frozen coffee thing they have here. When I walk in, I'm greeted by an enormous painting of a moose. I do a double take thinking I took a wrong turn and stepped into a hiking and wilderness store. Nope. It's a coffee shop, the fragrance that greets me leaves no question about that.

Why a moose?

There is a tiny redhead behind the counter taking orders. It only takes a few minutes before I'm up.

"Hi! Welcome to Mud House, what can I get for you today?" The tiny redhead asks so cheerfully.

"A medium Mocha Mud Puddle, please."

"Sure thing! It will just take a minute." She smiles so sweetly at me.

Out of the corner of my eye I see a young boy and a little girl sitting on the oversized couch, he's reading the girl a book. It's adorable.

"Do you have any?" The woman asks me as she hands me the drink. "Kids, I mean."

"Not yet, one day. I just started dating my girlfriend not long ago, I can see it happening but not quite yet." I admit, I probably should have told Kat that before this stranger. Oops.

"I got lucky with those two. Brady has been an incredible big brother to Daisey. He's her shadow, always looking out for her." I turn back to see her beaming, "I credit how amazing that boy is to his dads. The three of them are an amazing example."

A few moments later I'm walking out with the story of the moose, and I haven't been able to stop thinking about Kat. Even before the woman behind the counter told me the story, but even more so now. A Tesla pulls into the spot next to me, an older guy that looks like he hasn't slept in a month steps out and nods a greeting to me as I climb into my own car.

The drive back to Karma is short, we're only a mile away. When I step inside, I find Kat doing lunges with Ava. They're both laughing like a couple of hyenas when I walk in. They get along so well, it's comical. There are only a few members in here right now, no one is signed up for personal training until tomorrow so we're just here for moral support and to step in to spot as needed.

When Kat sees me her face lights up with the purest joy. Her eyes narrow in on the coffee and if possible, her smile grows even larger. She jumps to her feet and races over to me, her body crashes into me as her arms loop around my neck.

"Hi, Princess. I thought you might like this." I lift the cup to her lips, so she doesn't need to let go of me. Fuck she feels perfect against me.

"You are unbelievable and amazing, you know that?" She asks.

"Yes, but feel free to tell me again," I chuckle through my response.

She continues leaning onto my chest for several minutes until I'm not letting her drink fast enough for her liking. I smirk and press a soft kiss against her forehead before I loosen my hold on her so she can turn and lean into me while she drinks. We stand like that for a while just enjoying each other's presence. The smell of her cherry blossom shampoo lingers in the air around us. She smells divine. I softly groan when the front door opens. I release Kat and turn to say hello to the new arrival only to freeze. Kat steps around me to see who it is, and her body goes rigid.

A tall woman with jet black hair, ivory colored skin dotted with freckles and bright green eyes stands before us with the largest genuine smile splitting her lips.

"Hey sis!" Penny yells from where she stands at the door.

Chapter Twenty

What. The. Fuck.

My big sister is standing in front of me like no time has passed. Every emotion under the sun whirls inside me until it reaches the surface. I stumble on unsteady legs, falling backward into Clay's chest.

"Kat!" I hear Penny shout as Clay's arms catch me in a vice-like grip.

"What are you doing here?" I ask her, the question comes out all breathy.

"I wanted to check on you." She admits like it should be obvious, "I haven't heard from you since my last text. I needed to see you."

My eyes close as tears begin to fall. I'm so happy to see her, but I can't trust that she's here for the right reasons. Penny slowly approaches me, like she is walking on eggshells, waiting for me to break.

No, no. She's my sister. I can't think like that. Auggie wouldn't have told her if he didn't think it was safe. He doesn't speak to our parents after they originally disowned me, back when I first came out. My heart stutters in my chest as I keep my eyes locked on her. I feel Clay shift before he whispers into my ear.

"Let's go upstairs, you two can have some privacy."

I nod slowly. "Stay with me?"

We've been sitting around the living room for twenty minutes with no words passing between us. Clay is by my side on the couch, Penny is sitting in an armchair directly across from us. I don't know where to start. Where do I begin?

"Kat, I..." Penny starts. "I'm sorry. Not only for what happened when we last saw each other..."

She pauses, a tear falls down her cheek and my heart breaks in two. It takes everything inside me not to move to her side.

"I never apologized to you for this. I've just been avoiding it for the past twenty years." She's quiet and I have to strain to hear her. "I'm sorry I tried to kill myself. I'm sorry that you found me. I'm sorry I wasn't strong or brave enough to tell Auggie in time. He would be living such a different life now." She rushes out to keep me from cutting her off.

I stare at her. I'm not exactly sure what to say. Any time we've mentioned this, she's shut down. It's been over half of a decade since I last saw her. I had just turned twenty-one and I made the mistake of posting something on social media that our parents were able to put two and two together. I have since blocked her from everything and made all of my accounts as private as possible.

"Do you remember Garrison?" She pauses waiting for some sort of indication of whether I remember the person she's talking about.

"Wasn't that dad's friend from college who lived down the road?" I ask, my brain flooding with memories forgotten.

She nods, confirming my thoughts on who it was. He moved away not long after she tried to kill herself. I remember seeing a moving truck outside of his house the next day.

"He," She swallows hard, more tears are flowing now. "He raped me. Every day for a year," her admission has me crumbling. I cross the short distance between us and kneel in front of her, my hands holding onto hers tightly as she continues to tell me her story. "At first, it was just attention. I was popular back then; I didn't think anything of it." She scoffs at the memory, "but it escalated quickly. Instead of flirtation, it was quick touches that seemed innocent in the moment. When it happened the first time, I thought I was special. I thought I was grown up. A man wanted me. You know?" Penny pauses and squeezes my fingers which are still wrapped tightly around her hands. She sniffs back tears before continuing, "that first time it wasn't bad. After that though, he told me that everyone would be mad at me if I told them." She sobs through her words, "He told me everything a –an – and," she stutters as she tries to get through her memories. "Anything he could think of to force me into keeping my mouth shut." Her nails bite into my palms as she admits all of this to me. It's obvious the pain is still fresh for her, even after all these years. "Pen, I'm here. You don't have to…" I try to give her an out, she doesn't need to go on. I understand now.

"I need to. For you, for me. I need to tell you what happened." She forces out a resigned laugh. "I told him I didn't want to do it anymore. That I didn't want anyone to be upset with me." Penny shakes her head in disgust before she's able to share the rest. "He didn't like that, so he forced it. Every single day for a year, if I didn't find a way to get to him, he threatened you and he said he would tell Auggie which would make him hate me. It didn't stop until I tried to…" she lets her words die on her tongue. We both know what happened. What she tried to do; she doesn't need to say it again. "Auggie somehow figured it out when Garrison moved so abruptly. That's why he left home as soon as he turned eighteen. He's been trying to find him, to make sure he can't hurt anyone else." She glances next to me at Clay.

"Why are you telling me all of this now?" I'm so confused at these confessions. Don't get me wrong, I'm so very thankful but what happened that she wanted to tell me now, I don't understand.

"Auggie thinks they found him. That it's safe to tell my story, at least with you." She smiles half-heartedly. "Kat, I never meant to hurt you, not with this and not with…" she doesn't finish. "I honestly thought they were wanting to make amends since you were obviously in pain. I didn't know until after it was too late. I swear, had I known what they planned to say to you I would have fought it. Even if it meant a group home. I hate knowing that I caused you even more pain."

I raise onto my knees, wrapping myself around her middle. We sit there and cry together for a long time. A while later Clay clears his throat pulling us out of our bubble.

"I'm sorry, Penny, everything that you've been through is fucked. Christ, it's beyond the realm of fucked." He's quiet as he speaks. "But, with the guardianship. How are you here without them knowing?"

"Oh, well, Auggie sent me this phone to use in place of mine whenever I want to come see you." She holds up a simple black burner phone. "He had your number, his and a friend of his, Deke's, programmed. He's the one that brought me here. Auggie said Deke is the only one he would trust to keep me safe to get to and from the house."

The room falls silent again for less than a minute before she speaks again.

"So about Deke, he's kind of a dick." She and I share a look, and both laugh like little kids when one of us would say a bad word to get a rise out of our parents.

We sit and chat for a few more hours, catching up. I'm hesitant to fully trust her, but with what she's shared with me, I can't imagine she's got an ulterior motive. My heart hurts for everything she's endured, no one deserves what she's been through. At the same time, I'm terrified to fully let her back into my life.

It's after eight p.m. when Penny pulls out the burner and calls Deke to pick her up. I walk downstairs with her when he is close to the gym. Clay had gone back down a few hours ago to close for the night. He's sitting in the office when we come down the steps, sitting at his desk with his face scrunched in front of the computer.

"Babe, I'll take care of all of that in the morning. You're going to give yourself a headache looking at the screen like that." I laugh as gently lay my arms over his shoulders and press a kiss to his temple. "I'll be back in a minute; Deke is picking her up."

"I'll come with you," he insists and stands as soon as I step back. His hand is in mine as we stroll to the door with Penny next to me. Her arm looped around mine. The physical connection to both of them is a comfort in the crazy upheaval from the day.

"I will come see you again as soon as I can," she promises.

I don't get a chance to respond, a very large man walks through the front door of Karma. My heart stops, he's easily six-foot seven and huge. I mean really huge. The man puts The Rock to shame with how wide his chest is. The exposed skin of his neck and arms are covered in ink. Different images, some that look tribal, one that looks like Kelly Kapowski and another that resembles R2D2 cover the landscape of the skin I can see from here. When he sees Penny, his jaw clenches. He flattens his lips and just grunts a greeting. His hair is closely cut to his scalp, but he has a generous beard that makes him look even less approachable. I wonder if he used to be in the military. I shake my head, trying to piece all this together.

"Deke, my sister, Kat." Penny introduces us, "Kat, this is Deke. I told you he's a bit of a dick." She whispers that last part and winks at me.

"Uhhhhh, hi?" I'm so overwhelmed at the sight of this man that my own greeting comes out as more of a squeak. Don't get me wrong, I've worked with some big dudes, helping them buff up for one reason or another, but this. Wow.

After Penny and I exchange another hug, she and Deke leave the gym together. I stand in the silence for a few moments as I gather myself while Clay locks up. Suddenly, his warmth envelopes me again before he drags me out of my thoughts and leads me back upstairs.

Chapter Twenty-One

The way she looked at Deke like she wanted to consume him pissed me off. She all but drooled over the man, right in front of me. I'll admit, he was nice to look at and bigger than anyone either of us have worked with. Even so, she's mine.

I'm feeling annoyingly possessive, I know she isn't going anywhere, but damn. I groan and drag her back into my arms. I pull her flush against my chest and drag my hand down her chest to her pelvis, making sure she can feel my length on her ass.

"Princess," I growl into her ear. "You. Are. Mine."

I tilt her face to meet mine, my mouth crashing down on hers. I devour her, making sure she knows who she belongs to. She whimpers through the kiss, her ass grinding against my length. I don't want it to stop, but I also know that we have plans to go out tonight. I separate myself from her. She's panting with the fire of desire lit in her eyes.

"As much as I want to finish this, if we don't meet the girls for Hadley's birthday, they will show up here and have my ass." I chuckle.

"You're not wrong. Give me ten minutes. I didn't work up a sweat nearly as much as I expected today." She says before darting off back up to my apartment to get ready.

My eyes follow behind her, enjoying the view before she's out of sight.

We arrived at Finley's only twenty minutes later than planned. Everyone is here, even people I didn't expect to see. The older man I saw when I left Mud House is swaying back and forth with Hadley on the dance floor, Can't Help Falling In Love streams through the speakers. It's a little old school for Finley's but who am I to question the DJ when the birthday girl is happy.

"Hey!" Ryan runs up to Kat and me as we cross the dance floor to where our group is sitting. The redhead from The Mud House is chatting enthusiastically with a man and a second woman with a similar shade of the coffee lady's hair. I really need to learn names.

"Hey babe! Sorry we're late, I'll explain later." Kat half explains our tardiness to her friend. They share a quick embrace before Kat walks over to the three people I don't know.

"Alannah?!" Kat shouts; her voice full of excitement as she races over to the newest female of the group and wraps her in a tight squeeze. "I didn't expect to see you here! I probably should have since Had told us she was getting in touch with Connor. I'm so happy to see you!"

"Howya, of course I'd be here to celebrate Hadley's birthday." The woman I now know as Alannah replies, she's got a slight accent, but I can't quite place it.

"Clay, this is Connor's sister, Alannah. Alannah, this is my boyfriend, Clay." I don't miss the way she beams through the introduction which makes my heart and dick swell two sizes at once.

"Nice to meet you." I reply as Ryan waves the other two over to join us.

"Kayleigh, Liam, this is our friend Kat and her guy, Clay."

"Nice to see you again," Kayleigh smirks at me, "So you're the Mocha Mud Puddle?"

"Oh my god! Yes, I thought I recognized you. Your coffee is so good, it should be illegal!" Kat's fangirl reaction to realizing who Kayleigh is, is quite comical.

Liam chuckles and wraps his arms around Kayleigh's chest. "Have you tried her peppermint mocha muffins? I was a goner after she made those for me."

"Yes, so much so I have to have them on the menu year-round. They've actually become one of my top sellers." She tilts her head back, gazing into the man's eyes like he's the most incredible thing in her world. They share a quick kiss before turning back to the rest of us.

Hadley and Connor come over to the group when the song is over, once introductions are done with Connor and I, we sit and chat for a while. *Ah ha!* The accent I heard was Irish. Connor's is easier to place.

Kat leans into my side as conversation flows. Drinks are shared and we all get to know one another. This is my kind of birthday party, the smaller the better since I'm not one for large groups. Even this is pushing me a bit if I'm honest, but I'd do anything for Kat.

"Clay," Connor saying my name drags my attention from my own thoughts.

"What's up?" My eyes lock on his as I arch a brow.

"I wanted to thank you. Mo ghrá mentioned something you said to her when she was still in the hospital." He presses a kiss to Hadley's temple. "I just wanted to thank you for that."

"No matter what that motherfucker did, you are not defined by his actions or how you felt you needed to cope with it in a moment of weakness. You will heal and get on the other side of this, never doubt yourself. We're all here for you, day or night."

I smile as I remember the words I said to her that day and nod at him. I know he doesn't need a response. Alannah and Kat are chatting like they've been friends for longer than I've known her. I furrow my brow in confusion.

"Uh, how do you two know each other so well?" Hadley is the one who asks the question. "I'm not mad at it but, I didn't know y'all knew each other."

"I may have cornered her at the hospital to get a crumb of information about what was going on." Alannah speaks first.

"I didn't give her the specifics of why you were there." Kat interjects when Hadley's eyes widen.

"She was annoyingly protective of you. It was endearing." Alannah laughs, "we've been chatting since."

They both shrug at the same time and theentire table erupts into laughter. Our night continues as though we've all known each other for ages. Liam and Kayleigh share more stories about their kids, Alannah about her son, Sean. The rest of us chat about work and things we have planned for the coming weeks. When the clock strikes midnight, the girls make like Cinderella and turn into pumpkins.

Chapter Twenty-Two

Sweat glides down my face, back, and chest. My breaths come out in pants while I continue to move. My heart beats harshly against the walls of my chest as I go through the motions. It's not like I don't do this on a daily basis, but I find new ways to challenge myself to make sure I'm at peak performance level for both myself and my clients.

"Ten more reps, Princess." Clay taunts from somewhere behind me.

"Let me see you do this, Mr. I would rather jump rope every second of every day than do a single burpee for the rest of time." I throw back at him with a scowl.

When I finish my final double lunge burpee, I collapse on to the mats. Clay laughs as he tosses a towel at me before walking away. I wipe the sweat from my skin enjoying a moment of calm and the view of his perfectly sculpted ass before I have to continue with my day. My breathing and heart rate come back down to normal after several moments of rest and I sit up to take a few large gulps of water. My god, I needed to hydrate.

Once on my feet I walk over to the front desk to grab my phone and chat with Ava who is so deep in her studies she doesn't realize I've even approached. I smile, shaking my head, and just lean against the counter and scroll through my messages.

Alannah:

> Howya, love. Care to go out for a bite this weekend?

The next is my group text from Hadley and Ryan.

Ryan:

> Have you seen the guy Jax that is friends with Kayleigh and Liam? He's been at The Mud House the last few times I've been here.

Hadley:

> She's mentioned him to me, he's a playboy that has a stripper addiction babe.

Ryan:

> So, you're saying there's a chance I could have some fun?

Hadley:

> Oh. My. God. Kat! Where are you? Talk some sense into this girl.

Kat:

> Weren't you the one that told me to get the D? Get that D, Ry!

I chuckle as I press send on my response.

Penny:

> Can I come by for a few hours Saturday during the day? We can get lunch!

Kat:

> I'll clear my schedule for you, sis.

I scroll back up to Alannah's message and respond, knowing I need to talk to someone other than Clay about what's going on in my life and I'm just not ready to talk to Hadley and Ryan about it.

Kat:

> Absolutely. Your choice, my treat.

Alannah:

> How do you feel about CalMex?

Kat:

> You have my attention.

Alannah:

There is a place over in Ellicott that recently opened, 10th Ave Burrito.

Kat:

Sold. Saturday for dinner?

Alannah:

Can't wait!

Before I can fully enjoy the thought of having things planned for the next five days, a warmth envelops my back. The scruff of Clay's beard tickles my skin as he presses a soft kiss to the crook of my neck. I sigh in contentment, whenever I'm in Clay's presence, there is a calm that comes over me greater than I've ever known.

"Hey, Beautiful." He whispers, "I love seeing you drenched like this, but there are much more exciting ways to work up that kind of a sweat."

I chuckle and elbow him in the ribs. He doubles over, choking out a laugh. Ava chooses that moment to look up at us. Her eyes go wide in horror.

"What happened? Is everything ok?" She all but shrieks.

Clay and I are still laughing several minutes later when she gives up on us and goes back to her work. A group of women enter our space, led by no other than Leigh. Of course. I stand up, my mood no longer as light and carefree as it was only seconds ago.

"I guess that's my queue for cycling. How much would you kill me if I made innuendos throughout the entire class?" I turn toward the room I will be spending the next forty-five minutes in, my question still directed toward Clay.

"No matter what I say, you're going to do it anyway. Just make sure it's worth the backlash she's going to throw at both of us," he snorts before walking away.

"Pickle!" I hear the voice of my savior.

"I have never been so happy to hear that god forsaken name in my life." I turn toward Ryan. "Tell me you are here to join the class?

She glances over my shoulder and groans when she sees the devil woman. "You are so going to owe me."

"Have I mentioned how much I love you?" I snicker as I loop my arm around hers and drag her into the room with me.

"Hello ladies!" A sly smile twists my lips, "Who is ready to ride?" My tone lowers just a bit, Ryan chokes on a sip of water when she realizes what I'm doing and laughs at my rhetorical question.

"Ok, mount up and let's get started with a five-minute warm up, to get your blood pumping." I call out across the space and press play on my favorite warm up song, *I Had Some Help* by *Posty and Morgan Wallen* followed by *A Bar Song* by *Shaboozey*. It's the perfect amount of time for a warm up.

"Ok, Ladies!" I grin and wink at Ry who has the most mischievous smile splitting her face. "Let's make it hard today and work up a sweat until we're all dripping!" I press play on a list of every dirty but fast song I can think of.

The class goes by satisfyingly quickly. I feel proud of myself for every dirty thing said today, none of it was exactly inappropriate unless you were thinking dirty. By the time we're done and I step off of the platform my bike is stationed on, Ryan looks simultaneously like she's going to kill me and hug me.

"I have never hated you and loved you so much." She is giggling, "did you see her face? She looked like she was going to strangle the entire class."

Before I can respond, the she-devil herself approaches us.

"I will be speaking to Clay about how completely inappropriate you were today." She snarls at me.

"What do you mean?" I ask sweetly.

"You know exactly what I mean. That entire class should not have happened!" Leigh scolds.

"You seemed to enjoy it," I reply. "You seem to have worked up a good sweat, that's so great for your goals!"

She huffs and storms out of the room. Ryan and I exchange an amused glance before we walk out to watch the show. We barely enter the open space of the gym when we not only see, but hear Leigh losing her mind.

"Clay, that girl is so inappropriate. If you don't get rid of her, I will leave and take my friends with me. You will have no members left." She snarls.

"What was so wrong with the class, Mrs. Adams?" He asks in his customer service voice.

"She was making references to being hard and everyone dripping and don't get me started on the pumping comments!" She shrieks.

"I see." His owner's mask stays in place, but I can see the amusement in his eyes. He raises his gaze to find me and nods asking for me to join him. When I approach, she stiffens. "Kat, can you tell me exactly what was said today that Mrs. Adams is referring to?"

"I asked who was ready to ride, I mentioned we were going to make it a hard ride and that I wanted everyone to be dripping with sweat by the time we were done." My voice remains calm and professional even though I'm giggling inside. "Everyone seemed to enjoy the class, including Mrs. Adams, I've never seen her give it her all like she did this class."

"Alright, thanks Kat." Clay's response is clipped, and he motions for me to go back to what I was doing.

Chapter Twenty-Three

"**M**rs. Adams, I'm not sure what your agenda is when it comes to Kat, but I assure you, she is a professional." I try to smooth things over which just seems to push her even further.

"My agenda is that she is a bitch and shouldn't be left around the public unsupervised!" the woman snarls at me.

Are you fucking kidding me with this?

"Ma'am, if you speak about any of my employees in that manner again, you will no longer have a membership here." I respond cooly even though I can feel my calm begin to crack at its foundation.

"Just because you've finally – you know – doesn't mean you need to subject the rest of us to her shenanigans!" she snaps back. She looks proud of herself that she actually said that out loud.

"That's enough!" I growl, my professional voice and demeanor gone, causing her bravado to falter. I breathe heavily for several beats trying to find my calm even though rage is vibrating through my veins at her response. "I don't give two fucks who you are, Leigh, my personal relationship with her is none of your business. Nothing inappropriate has happened and I will not allow you to speak to or about Kat in that manner. You can get the fuck out, consider your membership terminated effective immediately. You will be refunded for the time you will not be using."

"Clay! You can't just... I have connections!" She stammers, realizing how badly she fucked up, "You'll regret this!"

"No, actually I would regret allowing you to continue coming into this space with how you act." I step toward her, forcing her to retreat backward, "If you don't leave right now, I will contact the police to escort you out. Because at this point, you're trespassing."

"You'll regret this!" She screams before turning on her heel and disappearing out the door.

Good fucking riddance.

A chorus of cheers erupts behind me. I turn to see the members that have been present are all on their feet roaring with excitement that the wicked witch is finally gone. I crow at the sight before me and have to hold back the urge to bow like it's my own encore response.

"Alright everyone, show's over. Go back to your workouts!" I shout and walk to my office where Kat is waiting for me.

She's perched on my desk when I enter, she doesn't meet my eyes for a moment. It's not until I close the door does she look up at me. Her emotions are etched across her face.

"I'm so sorry Clay, I didn't think she'd become that explosive." Kat's eyes are filled with unshed tears.

I close what little distance is left between us and cup her face with my hands. She flinches at the touch as if I would hurt her. I inhale her intoxicating scent. The beautiful blend that is uniquely her has my pulse coming back to normal. My lips find hers and press a soft kiss to each cheek and then her mouth. She whimpers at the connection; her body responds to mine so beautifully and so easily.

"Princess, I don't give a shit if you threaten her first-born son, no one will ever speak to you or of you in that manner." I tilt her face up to ensure she can see the sincerity in my eyes. "Do you understand?"

"Yes, but she can –" She starts but I don't give her a chance to finish it.

"She can suck my dick for all I care. I'm not going to be frightened by her when she was so very clearly in the wrong that the entire floor gave me a standing fucking ovation." I level her with a look.

"No." Kat's attitude changes drastically.

"No?" I repeat, but my confusion is apparent with the question.

"No, she can't suck your dick." A loud humph leaves her as she speaks.

I doubled over in laughter at her response, knowing too well that I felt the same way with how she was looking at Deke. I glance up at her again and it just restarts the laughter all over again. She's thoroughly unamused with my reaction.

"I don't find this funny, Clayton!" She drops my government name.

"Damn, Kat. Feeling feisty today, are we?" My amusement is still on full display from the look on her face, but I somehow get the laughter under control enough to pull her into me. She's pissed, her nostrils flare as I speak. "It was a metaphorical dick, Baby."

"I don't care, I'm not sharing," she pouts, arms crossed over her chest for good measure.

My lips find hers again, this time the kiss deepens, and she melts into me as I expertly work her over with my tongue. Kat moans and mewls into me as I coax her pleasure from our kiss. I step a bit closer to the desk so she can feel my length through my shorts at her center. I dig my fingers into her scalp, her teal hair feels like silk against my skin as I devour her mouth with my own.

I separate myself from her for just long enough to say, "You're the only woman I want or need in my life, Princess."

I go in for another kiss, but she backs away this time. She's panting, her eyes heavy and hooded with desire. The need is very much mutual but before I can make a move to take her right here there's a harsh knock on the office door. I groan with frustration and turn toward the intrusion palming my dick I squeeze trying to calm myself down with some sort of friction. I swing the door open and find Ryan standing out there, amusement dancing in her eyes.

"Sorry to interrupt you two but I had actually come by to talk to Kat before this all happened." She snorts.

"I don't like you very much right now." I sigh, stepping back to press one last kiss to Kat's puffy pink lips. "Later, beautiful," I wink at my woman before returning to the gym.

"Love you too, Clay!" Ryan calls after me. I flip her off and hear her cackle behind me.

I grin when I see Jenna and Tina entering. I cross the space, walking over to greet them. They're both looking at me like I have five heads.

"What the hell is that smile for? You're freaking me out." Tina's hesitance is comical.

"You just missed out on a show, but I also just got cock blocked by my girl's best friend. I'm smiling so I don't cry from blue balls." I shrug.

"What in the Grey's Anatomy friendship do those girls have?" Jenna snorts.

"I don't know what that means." I admit.

Tina snorts and drags Jenna away from me and the conversation.

Chapter Twenty-Four

Ryan is still drooling over Kayleigh and Liam's friend, Jax. From what Hadley said he's "bad news bears," but at the same time, who the hell are we to judge? Ryan says she just wants to have sex. I know it's been a minute for her. She's as bad as I am and hasn't truly dated since Greyson moved away. That was when they were kids, way before I knew her or Hadley. They were never actually together but she's had it bad for that man since she was a teenager. She's only slept around, refusing to get serious. I don't see why it's a big deal if she hooks up with Jax.

Though, unlike Hadley, I used to thrive with casual sex. She's never had a casual bone in her body. We really should have known better than to expect her to keep it casual with Connor. In our defense, the man is beautiful and with his accent, I don't hate when he calls me Pickle.

"Listen, babes. If you want to bang the man. Do it." I shrug as I take a seat in Clay's chair and grab a protein bar from the snack drawer. "Maybe don't broadcast it, or if you do, let us all watch because that would be hot." I wink at her.

"You perv." Ryan's giggle is infectious.

"Just because we ended our benefits doesn't mean I wouldn't enjoy seeing your body. You're sexy as hell, Ry." I pause as I rake my eyes up her tight body. "Even if you drive me crazy half the time, you're an extraordinary human that deserves everything you want. Don't settle for less. And for the love of God, make sure you get off!"

Ryan snorts, her body doubles over as she cackles. "Shit! Do you remember the last time I hooked up with someone? They were sexting me for days, getting me all worked up just to end up being a two-pump chump and I had to use a vibrator after, and he had the audacity to be offended that I didn't get off?"

"I will say," tears are streaming down my cheeks as we laugh together. "That was possibly one of the best calls I've ever received from you."

"I'm glad my pain could amuse you so, ass." She playfully thwacks my arm.

We're still laughing twenty minutes later when Clay walks back into the office but all he registers are my tears.

"What the fuck did you do, Ryan?" He snarls.

"Whoa, big man. Calm down. We were laughing," she pokes him.

"Why are you crying?" He tilts my chin up to face him.

I smile and stand, my hands loop around his neck and pull him toward me. Our lips crash together in a soft, quick kiss.

"We're good, I promise." I say against his lips before I pull away and wink at him.

"Ryan, as much as I adore you and respect your friendship with Kat, are you done? You interrupted something that I need to get back to." His eyes stay trained on me while he speaks to her.

"Wait, if you get to watch me, I want to watch you," she blurts out.

"Excuse me, what?" Clay stills against me.

"I'm teasing, big man. Although, I am curious to see what you're packing underneath those shorts." She teases before passing through the open doorway and closing it behind her.

Clays eyes burn into me with questions. "Should I be concerned? Jealous? Turned on? I'm not really sure what my brain is feeling but my dick is up for whatever you want, Princess."

"I mean, I wouldn't be against adding a third for a night or two, but not Ryan. That history is too complicated to share with you." I press my lips against his, begging for more. "So, what exactly were you wanting to get back to there...big man." I tease him with Ryan's nickname.

I'm finishing up with Tina and Jenna's joint session when I notice Penny walks in. Her long black hair is pin straight, cascading over her shoulders. A light green dress hugs her tiny frame, accentuating her soft curves, the color making her eyes pop. I wave at her and then notice that Hulk is with her. Oh good lord almighty that man is so large.

I don't respond when Tina asks me something that I absolutely don't hear. I realize they're both looking over their shoulders.

"Fuck me raw with a glitter dick, who the fuck is that." Jenna whisper-shouts.

"Bitch, don't bring Jasper into this." Tina responds quietly.

I furrow my brow confused by what Twilight has to do with this conversation.

"We have a glitter dildo that we named Jasper. Don't judge us." They both giggle at what must be a priceless expression on my face. "No seriously though, who the hell is that man? Is he related to Dwayne Johnson or something? Fuck me!"

"Shhh!" I urge them to stay quiet. "He's a friend of hers. He's just got a very threatening demeanor about him, and makes me nervous."

When our time ends, they say goodbye and walk in the opposite direction of me.

"Hey sis!" I smile and offer an air hug since I'm sweating. "Maui." I joke and nod toward Deke.

"No," is all he says and turns back toward the door. "Three hours, Ace."

She flips him off over the shoulder, which I swear I see his shoulders shake with laughter when she does it. Penny takes my hand leading me up to the apartment so I can wash up and change before we leave. I impress myself with how short a time it takes for me to get ready knowing I only have limited time with her.

My heart flutters in my chest as I sit down with my sister at a local diner. It's nothing fancy, but it's the first time we've sat down for a meal together since we reconnected. It feels so normal. Penny is glowing as she takes me in, a bright smile on her face. The hostess asks us for our drink orders immediately which is nice. She returns less than a minute later with our waters.

Penny looks like she's chomping at the bit to say something. I keep my gaze on her, waiting.

"I wanted to tell you something." She giggles.

Arching a brow I lift my drink to my lips.

"I am going to petition to have my need for guardianship re-evaluated." Her smile is filled with so much excitement and pride.

"Wait, is that safe?" I cringe at my own question. "I don't mean that you shouldn't be in charge of your own life. I just don't want to see you in a position that you're not ready for."

"No, I know that." She waves her hand like I didn't just make a jerky comment. "Auggie and I have been talking about it and he said that Deke will let me stay with him until I get my headspace under control."

"Sis..." I stare at her. Unsure how to continue. "Does he know the kind of responsibility that could entail?"

"Yes." She sighs. "He's seen a couple of episodes. I've asked him to pick me up just to get away from their house and he's helped coax me out of that state. He's not really that big of an ass, he's good to me."

A tinge of pink flares on her cheeks for just a moment. I don't call her out, knowing it's not good for her, but make a note to bring this up to Auggie as soon as possible. This could end in a dumpster fire.

Chapter Twenty-Five

Confusion and apprehension overwhelm me the more I run through Penny's potential escape plan. Could it work? Sure, but she could also end up getting into deeper trouble. What's not lost on me is if our parents find out they will absolutely have her thrown into one of those facilities she doesn't want to be in. They've wanted to hide away what happened to her, anything that makes our family look imperfect from the outside they must cover it up. When Augustus left, they acted like they had no son. When I came out to them being bisexual it was an entire ordeal of what it would look like for them. Granted they played it off like it was about me.

I sit on the couch with my knees tucked into my chest. I hold myself protectively while I wait for them to arrive home. My breathing has become heavier the longer I wait. I'm eighteen as of last month, and I'm leaving for college next week. They can't do anything to me if I tell them now. I've been repeating that to myself for the better part of the last month. I finally found the courage today to tell them. To get it off my chest and live my life as authentically as I can. Auggie should be here. He knows, he's known for years. Hell, even Penny knows, but she's too far gone to be of any emotional support for me right now.

A car door slams closed, and I hear a hushed conversation through the walls of our house and mom's high heels clicking on the sidewalk as she and dad walk closer to the house. I hear as the key enters the lock and a click tells me it's only a matter of seconds before everything changes. Mom is the first one who sees me. I'm sure I look like a hot mess express. I've been crying off and on, terrified of what they're going to do. But, my mantra has been keeping me sane or trying to at least.

"What's going on? Penny! Where is she? Is she ok?" My mother screams for my sister.

"Penny is fine, mom. I just need to talk to you and dad." I sigh, unsurprised at their initial concern being over Penny. "No one is hurt, everyone is safe and healthy. Can you sit down please?"

She stands there glaring at me before she speaks. "Why do you look like that?" she asks me with an accusatory tone. "Your face is red and splotchy. What is it?"

"Dad, can you sit down with us?" I try to pull my father into the conversation. They both sit on the oversized oak coffee table in front of me. Dad looks unimpressed, mom looks bored with my existence. None of this is new, you'd think I'd be used to it by now.

"What is it, Katrina? We don't have time for any of your nonsense." It's the first thing he's said to me all day, even though he had been home with me for three hours before they went out for dinner.

"I won't take up much of your time. I just wanted to tell you two something important. Something personal." I pause, waiting for them to acknowledge that this isn't going to be an easy conversation which they of course don't do. waiting for me to continue. "I'm bi." I spit it out like its poison.

"What do you mean? You're leaving? We know that honey, you're going to college." My mother laughs stiffly.

"No, mom. I'm bi, as in bisexual, as in I like men, and I like women." I admit the words out loud in a straight forward – pun not intended – manner for the first time in my life.

"No, you're not. You like boys." My mother states matter of fact.

"I do, and I like girls." I repeat myself.

She gasps. Her eyes fixed on me for several long beats before she opens her mouth to speak again.

"No, no you don't. No child of mine will be –," she whisper-yells the last part. "That way!" She sounds so disgusted. My father hasn't spoken since my admission, his face has turned beat red though. I'm nervous about what his reaction is going to be.

"Sorry to disappoint you, mom, but I am in fact, that way. You know Katie down the street? Mr. and Mrs. Donahue's daughter? I've gone out with her multiple times." I know I shouldn't tell them things like this, but my mother is being so awful to me that I just want to hurt her back.

"Enough!" My father's voice bellows over us. "No daughter of mine will be associated with that lifestyle. We did not raise you to be like this. How do you expect to live a life like this? To be happy? Have children? How do you expect anyone to take you seriously? You'll never be able to hold a woman's hand in public. People will look at you. Judge you. You'll just be a whore in their eyes."

I feel my stomach turning as I meet his gaze.

"Daddy, that's not how it works anymore. We have so many more rights now than we used to." I try to explain to him. "I don't even know if I'll end up with a woman. I just didn't want to go off to college without you and mom knowing!" I cry.

"That is how it works, Kat. Either you can change your tune, or you can go and pack all of your shit right now and go stay somewhere else until you are able to go to campus. I will not have a person of that lifestyle in my home." He growls at me.

"Daddy! I'm still your daughter, how can you do this?" I sob, tears stream down my cheeks.

"No, no daughter of mine will live like this." He snarls at me before stomping off only to yell back at me. "I will graciously give you an hour to pack up your life and figure out where the hell you're going to stay tonight."

I shake my head at the memories flowing so easily today. Shit. They are going to lose their minds when they find out that the only child they have left to control is about to leave them too. My heart hammers in my chest, threatening to beat its way out of my rib cage. "Howya! What's going…" The words die on Alannah's lips when she catches sight of my face. "What happened?"

Chapter Twenty-Six

My heart is racing when I take in Alannah's reaction. The expression on her face looks crushed for me, well for the me that no longer exists. Though, I guess I do in a way since it still affects me this much. I thought I was over it, but knowing what could possibly happen to Penny has me so anxious for her. I don't know if she really understands what she's likely to unleash.

"Ryan only knows a part of my past and that's just because we had been sleeping together." I admit once I've finished rehashing all my trauma to Alannah.

"And Clay?" She questions, there's no judgment in her tone, just curiosity.

"He knows everything. He met me at a dark time in my life when An – when she left me." I release a long breath, "I wouldn't have made it out of that without his support. When I left my parent's house, I had to use half of my savings to stay in a hotel because I didn't feel like I could tell anyone what was going on. If I had told Auggie he would have killed them. I didn't want that on his conscience." I laugh out loud at the last part.

"I'm so sorry, Kat. I can't imagine bearing the brunt of that experience on your own." She's been sitting next to me this entire time. Just now, she wraps an arm around my shoulders, hugging me to her side. "Sean came out to Connor and I recently and I was happy for him. To finally live his truth, to have the freedom to be who he is."

I feel a tear fall down my cheek.

"I don't mean to upset you. I just wanted you to know that's not how you should have been treated." She holds me tighter, "I'm bad at this, I'm so sorry."

"No!" I loop my own arms around her middle holding her as close as I can. "I'm not upset, it's the opposite. I love that you are so supportive of him. That parents like you really do exist." I smile even though she can't see my face.

We sit like that for a few minutes before we separate. Strangely, we have become so incredibly close in such a short period of time; it feels like coming home. But, the good kind of home, not my home, in case that wasn't obvious.

Our evening out turns into more of a cuddle session and trauma bonding while we drink cheap wine and eat terrible food. Alannah shares more about her husband and losing him so young. I can't imagine how I would react to that kind of loss. Even the thought of it guts me, to actually experience it? There's no way.

I find myself captivated by her stories. The way she's endured so much and has come out so much stronger than most people could. How she supported her son after her husband was killed. I wouldn't have the balls to do that. Sure, I'd watch but I couldn't do it. But...that's not my story to tell.

My body is covered in a sheen of sweat. I simultaneously groan and giggle when I open my eyes and realize Clay is all but laying on top of me. His arm and half of his chest lay over my middle, I carefully slide out from under him to relieve my bladder and make some coffee. I reach the kitchen and check the pot to find he already has it prepped and I just need to press start, which I do.

A few minutes after I'm back from the bathroom and the coffee is ready, I pour us both a cup, adding the vanilla flavored creamer to his and a splash of milk to mine before I carefully take them back to the bedroom. I set his on the nightstand closest to the side he deemed as his, which is closest to the door. And carry mine with me to my side of the bed which he is currently taking up two thirds of.

I snort as I sit up against the headboard and just enjoy the silence and closeness while I sip my drink. My mind still whirls from the night before and the conversation with Alannah and the conversation with Penny earlier in the day and all of my worries. There's no way I can get through this without reaching out to my brother.

I grab my phone from the bedside table and unlock it with my fingerprint. I scroll to Auggie's name and hover over the call button until I realize it's only five in the morning. Text it is, I tap on the message icon and start typing.

Kat:

> I don't know if you're awake but I need to talk to you. Do you know what Penny is planning? I've been so anxious over what is going to happen when they find out.

I press send and wait. A minute later a call comes through and I hit the screen to answer.

"Auggie." I breathe into the phone.

"Hey KitKat." I hear the smile in his voice.

"Do you know what's going on?" I repeat the question from my text.

"I do. I think it's going to be for the best. Deke is watching the house. If they try to take her anywhere, he will intervene." He sounds so much calmer than he should be.

"They kicked me out when I came out. If they find out she's in contact with me, there's no way they're going to give any warning." I let out an exasperated cry.

Clay starts to stir next to me, his arm finding me again and he locks himself around my thighs. I take a long sip of my coffee before placing it on the bedside table. My fingers find his hair and I drag my hands through the wild mane.

"I know more than you think which is why I'm pushing so hard for this." He admits, the venomous tone he exudes startles me. "Trust me when I tell you they will pay."

"Aug, no!" I cry, knowing what he is planning without the verbal confirmation from him.

"I've gotta go, I'll talk to you soon, KitKat." His voice is back to the sweet big brother I know. "I love you, sis."

The line goes dead and I'm sitting here annoyed. An angry groan leaves my lips and Clay stirs again.

"Good morning, Princess." He tightens his hold on me. The raspy morning voice sends heat directly between my thighs.

And just like that, my worries are forgotten, if at least only temporarily.

Chapter Twenty-Seven

S ix Months Later

Johnny's face is red as he finishes the final lap on the push sled. Excited to see he's maxed out at thirty pounds. The push sled is no joke, and he has been trying to get to his max since he decided to bulk up a few months ago. I've been crouched down to be eye level with his hips as he's been pushing the sled.

"I'm gonna miss you man." He declares as he stands to his full height.

I shoot up from my position closer to the floor at his words.

"Shit, she gave you a date?" I ask.

"Yep, in three weeks." Johnny says and takes a generous sip from his water bottle as his eyes lazily roam across the room before it lands on something. Or someone.

"Damn, man." I stand there in silence unsure of what to say.

"Don't get all mopey on me. I'll still see you up until I leave. What's the chance I can pay you to keep training me and move back with me?" He chuckles.

"Sorry man, nothing is going to take me from Kat." I smirk as my eyes wander over to the direction where he's staring to find Kat and Hadley are working together with free weights. We watch the two of them for a few moments with no words passing between us.

He clears his throat and breaks the silence. "I don't blame you. Listen, I've got a client meeting. I need to get a shower and change. I'll see you later tonight, yeah? And let's do lunch next weekend" Johnny claps his hand on my shoulder before disappearing into the locker room behind where we stand.

As disappointed as I am that my time with one of my best friends is coming to an end, I can't help but smile. My gaze still trained on Kat, as she and Hadley laugh together which only makes my heart full. She's happy, happier than I've seen her in a long time. To think I had something to do with that, it brings me such contentment. I feel so lucky to be just a part of her reason for this much joy.

The moment Kat's eyes land on mine, time stops. Her cheeks flush letting me know just how much I affect her, even from across the room. A playful smirk dances across my lips as I wink at her before turning to check my schedule with Ava.

She is on a call as I approach. Instead of waiting, I walk around the back of the counter to grab the printed calendar for the day only to be surprised to see my calendar is clear for the next hour. It's unusual for me to have a break in the middle of the day, I can't say I'm disappointed though.

Before anyone can stop me, I head back to the office and climb the stairs to my apartment. Quickly crossing the distance to the kitchen, I grab a bowl from the cabinet and a bag of pre-made salad from the top shelf. My lips turn up at the corner when I feel her presence behind me.

"Hey, Princess." I say as I stand back to my full height and turn toward her.

"How do you do that?" Kat's giggle is infectious.

Instead of responding, I close the distance between us and cage her against the counter. My lips find hers for the briefest of moments before I pull away and press my forehead against hers. Kat's soft whimper makes me chuckle.

"What's up?" I ask while I return to my salad and sit to eat.

"Hadley is having a birthday party for Connor next weekend. She wanted to know if you could come too." She asks as she walks to the fridge to grab a snack.

"Shit, I just made plans with Johnny. He's moving back to help with his family business back in Chicago." I stand to pull her into my arms. "I'm sorry, Princess."

Her face flashes with disappointment for just a second before she presses a soft kiss to my lips before pulling away with a mischievous smirk. "You'll make it up to me later."

My lips twitch at the corner as I try not to react.

"And how do you want me to make it up to you?" I muse as I return to my seat at the table.

Kat doesn't speak as she closes the distance between us, she bends at the waist in front of me and slides my bowl just out of reach before she takes its place. She turns quickly and hops onto the table and sits before me. A wicked smile plays on her lips as she leans in and presses her lips against mine. When she sits back up and places her hands on either side behind her, bracing herself she arches a brow with a question that doesn't need to be voiced aloud.

My chest rumbles with a deep chuckle. I reach for the waistband of her yoga pants and drag them down her sexy toned legs. Once they're around her ankles I dip my head and dart my tongue out to swipe along her seam before settling on her sensitive bundle of nerves.

A powerful bass greets me as I enter Finley's later that evening. Johnny is sitting on a stool in front of the bartop, his head in his hands. My feet are moving before my brain can catch up. As soon as I approach, he glances up long enough for me to see his eyes are red like he's been crying.

"Johnny, man. What's up?" I ask cautiously.

"Fuck man, I –." He shakes his head. "I did something. I don't regret it, but I did something."

"Ok…" I keep my eyes trained on him while I wait for him to expand.

Johnny doesn't say anything for several long moments, another voice pulls me out of the conversation that I'm waiting for. My glance darts in the direction of the voice, Haley, the waitress from the last time we were here is bartending tonight.

"Hey sweetheart, what can I get you?" She's leaning against the bar giving a direct line of sight to her breasts.

No thanks.

"I'll take a Moscow mule," I nod at her before turning back to Johnny. "I'm gonna need more, dude."

"I can't." He blows out a long-drawn-out breath. "Just make sure the Irishman takes care of Hadley once I'm gone."

"What the hell are you gonna do?" I shove his shoulder and force him to face me. "You're being evasive and it's fucking weird."

A darkness clouds his usually bright eyes when he meets my own, an unspoken threat that has me backing down. *What the fuck.* Johnny raises his hand to get Haley's attention once again and orders a Whiskey Long Island. The man is set on getting trashed if that's his drink of choice. Jesus.

The rest of the evening goes smoothly, his mood shifts to what it usually is. Though, he doesn't bring up whatever the hell had him so torn up when I first got here. By the time we're ready to go, he's too trashed to drive and I only brought my bike. When I finish my search through his pockets to find no keys, I realized just how fucked we are. I fish my phone from my jeans and send a text.

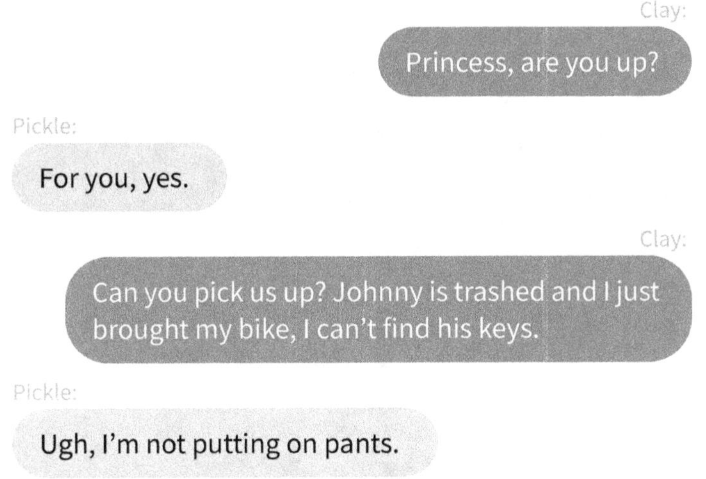

Clay:

I swear, if you show up without pants I'm going to take you over my knee.

Pickle:

See you soon. (wink emoji)

Chapter Twenty-Eight

Hadley has been gone for three hours with no word. She's with her lawyer, Danielle so nothing could be wrong, right? No, not right, everything could be going wrong. She went to see Andy to ask for a divorce again, this time in person. Sure, he's in jail now but what does that matter when the person she is seeing is as crazy as he is.

When Had told us her plan, going to ask for a divorce in person, it seemed like an understandable thing to do; her lawyer will be there, and Connor wouldn't let anything happen to her. Plus, Andy would be able to sign it immediately. However, when Hadley informed us that she wouldn't be telling Connor, that made us a bit anxious.

Ry and I started on a circuit in Karma but that lasted all of ten minutes before we both lost our damn minds and came upstairs to drink. And that's where we've been for the last almost three hours. Hadley was supposed to text us when she got there, which she did. She was also supposed to let us know when she was going in, but we haven't heard from her since.

"Are you sure you don't have Danielle's number?" I ask Ryan for the third time as I pace the length of Clay's living room.

"Princess," I hear his smooth whiskey voice behind me and turn toward the sound that calms me. "Breathe, baby, she's ok."

"Ok, but how do you know that? Have you heard from her? Why would she call you and not us?" I rush out as my feet continue carving out a path in the floor.

"Whoa," Clay quietly chuckles.

"Exactly. We're both spiraling." Ryan says from where she's sitting on the couch with her knees pulled into her chest.

"Unless you hear something negative, try to breathe. He's not going to be able to try anything." Clay tries to break through to us as both Ryan and my phone's ding with a text notification.

Connor:

> Howya ladies. Is Hadley ok? She's not responding to my messages.

Fuck.

I groan and show Clay the text. He snorts and takes the phone from my outstretched hand before tapping furiously on the screen and hands it back. When I read what he sent my chest heaves as I take in a deep steadying breath.

Kat:

We're fine Con, her phone died. She'll message you when she can.

I toss my phone onto the couch next to Ryan like it's venomous and start to pace again. Strong hands grab hold of my arms holding me in place. I look up into the honey gaze that has been a balm to my soul for years. Clay's hands grip my hair forcing my eyes to stay locked on his.

"Princess, breathe. You're going to make yourself hyperventilate if you keep this up." Clay's forcefulness drags me out of my anxieties, at least a little. He pulls me down to sit on his lap. Strong arms wrap around me like a vice until I catch my breath.

"Thank you," I breathe out once I'm able to find my voice again.

A second later a pained groan sounds from down the hallway. The three of us turn to the direction of the noise to see Johnny stumbling toward us on unsteady feet wearing only a pair of boxers. I do a double take at what looks like a third leg when he groans again and drags his large hand down his unshaven face. I dart my eyes to the floor to avoid direct eye to dick contact.

"Why are you people so damn loud this morning?" He groans while he blindly heads to the kitchen.

"Nice morning...wood, Johnny." Ryan teases him.

"What?" Johnny asks and looks down at the tent pitched below his waist. "Shit" He growls and then stands tall. "Fuck it, we're all adults. If you want to see it let me know, Ryan."

"Yep, that's not happening here. You can drive him home if you want to see it, Ryan." Clay groans from behind me as he buries his head in my neck which makes me giggle. "Not funny, Kat."

"It's kind of funny." I press my face into his neck, breathing in his mouth-watering scent. "By the way, Johnny. It's one in the afternoon." Ryan giggles as she saunters into the kitchen with him.

Clay and I sit in silence for a moment before the sound of Ryan's loud gasp pulls our attention to where she and Johnny are standing together.

"Oh my god! You did not! Ryan!" I scold my friend while doing my damnedest to bite back the laugh.

"Kat! Come look at this! It's pierced!" Ryan squeals as she's got the band of Johnny's boxers pulled away from his chiseled stomach so she can see his dick.

"Absolutely not. The only cock she's seeing is mine." Clay growls and holds me even tighter, which I didn't think was possible.

"Yea, I don't want to die, but you can play with it later, Ry." I hear Johnny's gruff voice say to my friend. "What are you guys doing sitting around like this anyway?" He asks as he sits down on the couch with his large hands wrapped around a mug of fresh steaming coffee.

"Hadley went to see Andy and we're freaking out because we haven't heard from her." Ryan explains.

"Ry! Shut up, he's Andy's lawyer!" I whisper-shout at her.

Before anyone else can speak, mine and Ryan's phones ding with a text notification.

Hadley:

> I just sent him a message. It's done. I need to see him, then I'll call you two later.

My body relaxes when I feel a whoosh of air release from my lungs. Clays arms cradle me against his chest as the adrenaline finally starts to drain out of me. Suddenly I feel exhausted.

"Princess. Why don't we lay down for a bit so you can relax?" His voice is so soft I barely hear it.

"Yea, I'll take Johnny home. I feel like I could use a nap myself." Ryan's voice cuts through the haze in my head.

When my gaze lands back on Ryan, she's standing next to Johnny who is now dressed in what he had on when I picked him and Clay from the bar last night. I drag my hands down my face to clear the confusion. When the hell did he get dressed?

"Love you babe, I'll talk to you later." Ryan calls as she descends the stairs to get outside. "I'll keep her distracted for you," I hear Johnny say before he disappears down the stairs behind Ryan, closing the door behind him.

For the love of God.

Chapter Twenty-Nine

Clay has me on all fours as his nails bite into my flesh as he holds onto my hips while he saws into me. The room is filled with moans of pleasure as he reaches around and presses against my clit. I cry out and push my hips back to meet his thrusts. My fingers dig into the sheets, my need for more of this man is something out of a romance book. Fuck, I can't get enough.

"That's it, Princess. Give me what I want." I hear Clay's throaty pants as he fucks into me harder with each thrust.

My cunt convulses around his thick length at his demand. I shatter around him as he continues to fuck me through my orgasm. Clay's cock grows even more inside me before his movements become erratic as he finds his release with my name on his lips. We both collapse on the mattress, panting for several moments until we catch our breath.

"Fuck, beautiful. You're going to be the death of me." Clay rolls onto his side. His arms wrap around me, and he drags me into his chest.

I giggle briefly until my phone starts to ring. I glance at the time, realizing its' three in the morning. Who would be calling me this early, I ponder. Clay hands me my phone from the nightstand he happens to now be closest to which is where I left it when we laid down this evening. I sit up when I see Connor's name on the screen. My finger swipes to answer the call and I bring the device to my ear.

"Connor? Is she ok?" I rush out, the organ in my chest pumps so hard I can hardly hear over the sound of my heart.

"That's difficult to say. Sorry to call you so early, Kat." He pauses. His voice is soft and full of emotion. "Andy was killed tonight. She's asleep right now but can you come over, so she's got all of us when she wakes up? Ryan is already on her way."

"Shit, I'll leave in ten minutes." I say in response before disconnecting the call. I collapse onto the mattress taking a moment to wrap my head around what Connor just told me.

"What's going on?" Clay asks, his body has gone rigid.

"Andy's dead. Killed." I explain as I turn to face him. His eyes go wide, he's as shocked as I am. "Hadley is understandably upset so we're going to Connor's. Ry is already on her way, so I have to go." I stand from the bed; Clay's eyes track me as I pace back and forth trying to find something to wear.

"Baby, go wash up, I'll grab your clothes." He offers while he stands and faces me in the direction of the bathroom.

My mind is going a million miles a minute while I quickly go through the motions of washing up. What my grandmother used to call a bird bath, though my mom always called it a hooker bath. Right now, I feel like the latter description is a better fit, having just had sex and now with the news, I'm forced to rush out.

Connor gave up on sleeping in his bed an hour ago when he realized just how close to a Grey's Anatomy scene this was. Ryan and I are cuddled up on either side of Hadley's sleeping form. Ready to do whatever she needs as soon as she wakes.

Hadley starts to stir and then stiffens when she senses us.

"I love him for calling you two but one of you still smells like sex," she groans, her eyes popping open into slits. They land on me, and she arches a brow. "Is the dick good?"

"Hadley!" I scold, my cheeks flush red with heat.

"I need to think of literally anything else, so please." She sits up, her knees slowly slide into her chest as she makes herself smaller.

"Ok, fine. It's the best dicking I've ever had. It's hard to even get through a day at Karma without ..." I glance out to the hallway, still not ready for Connor to hear this. " – messing around. That office has seen my bare ass more than the locker-room showers have if I'm honest."

"Babe, I love you so much. But I hate you so much more." Ryan whines next to Hadley. "I didn't even get into Johnny's pants. Even after him showing me his dick at Clay's."

"Wait, Johnny? As in Andy's lawyer, Johnny?" Hadley sits up straight.

"Yeah, he got wasted the other night when he was out with Clay. I had to pick them up." I pause contemplating if I should continue before I do, "and he was there the day you went to get the papers signed."

"Yea, and he has a piercing." Ryan whisper-shouts.

"Wait, how do you know that?" Hadley turns toward Ryan with confusion. A giggle passes my lips before I can stop it.

"He was hard, and I was curious, so I asked him to see it." She shrugs like it's no big deal.

We stay in bed and talk for a while about everything from Clay, Johnny and Connor, to the elephant in the room. It takes some convincing before she confides in us, but as always, we don't keep secrets from one another. After an hour of chatting Connor comes in with a tray of breakfast for the three of us.

"Wait, when did you leave to get Mud House?" Hadley asks him when she takes her first sip of coffee.

Connor's cheeks tinge pink as he speaks. "I asked Kay to have some delivered."

Hadley moves the tray in front of Ryan before she stands and walks on the bed toward her man. She leaps into his arms where he wraps himself around her. "I love you, baby."

"Mo ghrá," It's a whispered response but Ryan and I share a smile when we hear it. Their relationship is so inspiring, it started in the most unconventional way and yet they're stronger than ever.

"Aw, I love you guys." Ryan teases them from her spot on the bed as she lifts a peppermint mocha muffin to her lips. "Oh my god, I love these more," she moans around the bite.

"Beautiful, Alannah is here. Do you mind if she comes in to talk to you?" Connor's somber tone catches my attention.

"Of course. We don't have to stay in here. I'm not broken, I'm just. I don't know how to explain it." Hadley's response is quiet. "I'll meet you two in the kitchen. Bring the muffins, don't eat all of them, Ry!" She calls over her shoulder as she leaves the bedroom.

Chapter Thirty

"Hey beautiful!" I call to Alannah, who is sitting at the dining room table with Hadley. She smiles warmly at me before standing to greet me.

"Hey Kat," her Irish accent being so less obvious than Connor's still amuses me.

We share a quick hug before Ryan comes out with the tray of breakfast and sets it on the table for the four of us to share. Ry pours a fourth coffee and places it in front of Alannah before she takes a seat herself. There are several moments of silence until Alannah finally speaks again.

"Hadley, I don't know what all Connor has told you about my Colin before he died," She pauses to take a sip of her coffee. "We were young when we got married, even younger than you and Andy were." I sense her sadness and place a hand on top of hers, "I hadn't told anyone, not even Connor about this until a couple of years ago. Obviously, you know my brother, he wasn't happy. Colin had an alcohol and gambling addiction. The night I confronted him and told him I wouldn't continue to support his habits, he hit me. It was only the one time; I know now I should have left but I stayed for Sean."

"Oh my god, Lan!" Hadley gasps and rushes over to Alannah's side.

Alannah squeezes Hadley's hand as she continues. "He was drinking the night of the accident. It happened on his way home from an underground casino." Alannah chuckles darkly. "He had borrowed too much from a loan shark and they cut his brakes. The girl that hit him was drinking too. So, the police didn't look too far into it."

"Lan, I'm so sorry." Hadley whispers as she continues holding Alannah's other hand.

"No, no. I'm fine now." She offers a sad smile. "I'm telling you this so that you know you're not alone. It's a weird feeling being sad but thankful that a toxic person is out of your life."

"Fuck." Ryan whispers, her eyes wide as she takes in the sight before her. Alannah and Hadley hold each other, having a shared trauma neither of us could possibly understand.

"I've realized after a lot of time and reflection; my sadness was because of Sean losing his father." She takes a deep breath, "Take time, but do not ever feel bad that you are sad about this loss. No one has a right to tell you how to feel. Not even my bossy big brother."

"Hey!" Connor calls from the hallway where he's apparently been eavesdropping.

"That's what you get for listening to a private conversation brother." Alannah's tone is much lighter now as she teases Connor.

The mouthwatering aroma of freshly brewed coffee greets us as Hadley, Ryan, and I enter Mud House. Ryan and I stand in line while Hadley runs to the restroom before she orders. Kayleigh is all smiles behind the register as she takes order after order.

"So, are we going to talk about the elephant in the room?" Ryan asks when Hadley rejoins us.

"What are you talking about?" Hadley and I ask in unison, we exchange an amused expression.

"Jinx! You're buying the coffee!" I announce with a wicked giggle.

The three of us are rolling in laughter by the time we reach the counter to see Kayleigh.

"Hey! How are you sweetie?" Kayleigh's question is directed toward Hadley.

"It's hard to explain, but better than I had been. Thank you for asking and thank you for the delivery too. That was so sweet!" Hadley replies shyly.

"Anything for Connor. My daughter would have my head if I said no to anything her favorite uncle asked." Her lips turn upward into a bright, beautiful smile. "Just don't tell Jackson, he'd be upset that he's no longer the favorite." She stage-whispers.

The three of us laugh with her, I haven't met Jackson, so I have no idea who she's talking about; but Ryan has a look on her face like she knows a lot about the man. Once we place our orders we step to the side and wait for our drinks. Kayleigh is quick and has everything ready in a matter of minutes.

Hadley leads Ryan and I to the couch and oversized armchairs in the center of the cafe's lobby. I grin at the resemblance to Central Perk. Damn, Rachel Green was one of my first biawakening moments. I groan at the memory. Jennifer Aniston could still get it. God I'm worse than a damn man.

As soon as we take our seats the energy in the entire place shifts. I glance around to see what could have caused it, which is when I notice Hadley's eyes are glued to the entrance. My eyes follow the direction she's facing when I see a woman with a car seat carrying what must be an infant.

"Hadley, what's wrong?" I ask, she doesn't answer, and so I try another question. "Who is that?"

"Naomi." She whispers. And the moment the name leaves her lips the woman's gaze is trained on Hadley.

She saunters over or at least tries to saunter over with her arm looped around the handle of a car seat. A disgusted expression is plastered on the woman's face. I stand, placing myself between my friend and the woman who caused so many problems for her relationship with Andy.

"No, Naomi. It's not happening." I snarl at her as quietly as I can to keep the other patrons from what she's looking to accomplish.

"No, what? No, I can't talk to the woman who killed my daughter's father?" She screams.

"Oh, hell no. Bitch, please. You were sleeping with her husband, he ended up in jail for his own stupidity and probably pissed someone off. It's not her fault. Take a seat or leave." The harsh reaction comes from Ryan who is nearly foaming at the mouth and ready to pounce on Naomi.

"No, absolutely not. I don't know who you think you are, coming into my place of business like this, Naomi, but it's not happening," Kayleigh snaps out in her best mom voice. Naomi's eyes widen a fraction as my friend continues. "Yeah, it's not hard to figure out who you are. I will not tolerate this kind of behavior. Get. Out. Now." Kayleigh points a finger toward the door as she narrows her eyes.

"Whatever, I'll see you at the reading of the will, where I'll get his money. Bitch." Naomi growls in Hadley's direction.

"Shit, I'm going to need something stronger than coffee after that." Kayleigh groans. "Tequila, anyone?"

The girls and I follow Kayleigh back to her office. We make ourselves comfortable between the small couch and chairs surrounding the space. Hadley and Ryan flop back on the couch while Kay and I take the desk chairs. My gaze has been locked on Hadley since Naomi's grand entrance. She hasn't fallen apart which has me anticipating an intense downward spiral.

"So, that was Naomi." Kay breaks the silence as she grabs a few carryout coffee cups from behind her desk along with a stunning baby blue bottle with a cork stopper from the drawer. The white label reads Don Julio, I've never been a tequila drinker so I'm not sure what to expect.

"The one and only, and with his daughter." Hadley breathes out as she takes the cup from Kayleigh's outstretched hand. Ryan and I take our cups next and then Hadley speaks again.

"Fuck this, I didn't do a damn thing wrong here. I'm not going to get in my feelings over any of them." She holds her cup out, the universal signal to *cheers*. "Fuck Andy, this is my life and I'm living it for me."

The four of us shout our praise at her declaration before we all shoot back the warm liquid. The burn is nice, it's no pickleback but it's not bad. I swipe my tongue across my lips to make sure I don't miss a drop when I realize Hadley is gagging.

"What the hell did you just give us, Kay? Gasoline?" Ryan asks as she coughs while patting Hadley's back.

"Ah, your first time?" Kayleigh asks them as she winks at me with a sly grin.

Based on their reaction it's going to be the last time.

Chapter Thirty-One

One year later

That day a year ago really solidified our friendship with Kayleigh, we try to include her as much as possible and it's been an incredible ride. She's become a core part of our lives, her entire family really. To this day, it amazes me how she and Liam live with her ex and his husband without any issues. My parents could never, though they're a special case in an entirely different way.

A warm breeze washes over me as I step outside of Karma to wait for Ryan to pick me up. I'm dressed in a pair of dark jeans and a short sleeve scoop neck black top. The neck isn't plunging, we're going to a child's birthday party after all. I'm stylish, yet I feel comfortable, that is until Ryan pulls up with a car full of gifts.

"What the heck did you do?" I gasp, "I was going to just give her a card with cash! Now we'll have to stop at a toy store on the way. You can't out gift me!"

Ryan's giggle is infectious as I slide into the passenger seat. "Babe! We have to outdo Jana, of course I went bat shit and bought everything in the store I thought she'd like."

Crap, she's right.

"Fine, let's go drop my savings on the kid." I groan and I buckle my seatbelt.

We pull up to a huge stone house an hour later than we planned. Kayleigh and her family have a gorgeous home, I mean it would have to be if it was going to fit all six of them, right? Hopefully they won't be too mad at us for showing up late since the party started thirty minutes ago. It could be worse; Ryan's Jeep is filled to the roof between the two of us. We may have gone a bit overboard. *Just a bit.*

Once we're parked on the street in front of their house, Ryan turns the key to switch off the ignition. We both push open our doors and slide out, holding a large present in our arms. The gifts are so big we have trouble seeing around them. Once we find our way to the house, the front door opens before we have a chance to ring the bell. I hear a familiar voice from the open doorway.

"Son of a bitch! Kay!! I'm going to have to go back to the store" Jana, Kayleigh's best friend groans, "Come on in She Hulk one and two."

"What are you talking about?" Kay's sweet voice sounds from further away as we walk inside and place the big packages on the hardwood floor as soon as we enter. "Holy shit! What did you do?"

"Jar!" a voice yells from somewhere in the house.

"So, we're a tad competitive," Ryan announces, "and well. We've got to outdo Jana; she's already had so many birthdays we wanted to make sure the kids liked us considering how close they already are to Hadley and Connor."

"Oh no you don't, you're not going to blame us," Hadley joins us in the foyer. "They mean well, I should have warned you." She laughs.

"Liam, Joel!" Kayleigh yells for her current husband and ex husband toward the living room where everyone is chatting while they've been waiting for us. She's got her arm looped around Jana holding her in place. "I'm going to need you to unload a car."

"Jana!" The guy's groan in unison.

"Absolutely not, this one wasn't my fault." Jana throws back at them. "And with how hard she's holding onto my arm, she's not going to let me fix that." she pouts.

Liam and Joel appear with Lance and Connor on their heels. Connor grins at us as he pulls us in for a hug one at a time.

"Howya, Pickle? Howya, Ryan?" His brogue is thick this afternoon.

"Holy fuck!" Lance, Joel's husband, yells as soon as he steps out and sees just how full the Jeep is.

"There is going to be so much money in the jar today!" Kay and Joel's son, Brady's voice breaks the tension from where he sits in the living room with his sister.

Being that we have four men here, the gifts are all brought inside in one trip. So it wasn't that bad. Right? Right.

As soon as everyone is back inside another car speeds up to the house in a nice black sports car. Damn, that's a gorgeous piece of machinery. I elbow Ryan in the ribs to get her attention.

"Ouch! Use your words!" She whines and rubs where she felt the impact. I nod toward the driveway and her lips turn into a wicked grin. "That must be Liam's best friend, this is going to be fun."

I shake my head with a suppressed chuckle before I walk in the direction which everyone else has disappeared. I find Brady playing a handheld video game while Daisey, Kayleigh and Liam's daughter, is being followed around by a cluster of tiny humans that I haven't met yet. Crap, I barely know how to talk to Daisey and Brady, I don't do kids, it's why I bought gifts. Sure, I want my own someday, but they'll be easier to hang out with because they'll belong to Clay and me, right?

My heart starts beating quickly in my chest at the overwhelming what ifs going on in my mind at the moment. A gentle hand presses against the small of my back which startles me back into the present. With a jolt, I turn to see Hadley standing at my side with a look of concern on her face.

"What happened?" I ask as I glance over her shoulder for Connor who is staring in our direction, but he doesn't look concerned.

"That's what I was coming over to ask. You look like you were having a panic attack." She says softly.

My breath catches as Daisey and her friends rush back in and run toward the backyard again. Hadley smiles at the kids briefly before her gaze returns to me. As if a light bulb goes off on her head she nods.

"Are you?" She asks.

"What? No! Of course not. I was just thinking..." I pause for a few minutes before I can find the words to go on, "I've never been good with kids. Is it going to be different if they're ours? Or am I going to bring children into this world and not know what I'm doing? What if they hate me?"

Kayleigh must have snuck in while I was in my own head because her voice startles me when she speaks. "I hate to break it to you sweetie, but I don't think anyone knows what they're doing when they bring children into the world. They just take it a day at a time." She laughs quietly more to herself than to me. "The fact that you're concerned about the what ifs when you're not pregnant says you're going to be an incredible mom."

"Thank you" I reply and pull both Kayleigh and Hadley into my arms.

"Aw yea, I want in on that action." A deep velvety male voice announces from behind us.

"I love you Jax, but absolutely not in this lifetime." Kayleigh groans and shoos us out of his general vicinity.

It doesn't go unnoticed, at least not by me, that Ryan is hovering around Jackson with her chest pushed out as far as she can manage. I cock a brow in her direction, and she waves her hand at me to mind my business. My lips twitch into a grin as I shake my head. She deserves a little fun in her life.

"Kay, what's his deal?" Hadley asks Kayleigh as we reach the back patio where the youngest are playing and the guys are keeping an eye on them.

Kayleigh motions for us to take a seat on the gorgeous black and gold wicker furniture. It surprises me how comfortable it is, given its outdoor furniture. Once we're all situated Kayleigh explains.

"He's not had a girlfriend in all the years that I've known him. Brady is nine now, so it's been about four years." She takes a breath, "Listen, I love him dearly. He is an incredible friend to Liam and he's fantastic with our kids."

"There's a but coming," I tease.

"He's got a stripper addiction. He's calmed down quite a bit since Liam and I got together but it's still extremely frequent." She shakes her head before she continues further. "He will hook up with every dancer at a club and then go to a different club and start over again. It's to the point that he has to drive two hours one way to get to a club he hasn't been through already."

"Do you really think he'd sleep with Ryan then if she's not a dancer?" Hadley asks the question without hesitation.

"Honestly, I don't know. Just make sure she's not expecting a happily ever after. I don't think the man knows what monogamy is." Kayleigh groans.

"Who doesn't know what mono-moose is, momma?" Daisey, Kayleigh and Liam's daughter asks as she climbs into her mom's lap.

"Oh boy, here we go again." She laughs.

Chapter Thirty-Two

S everal days later I'm at Karma working on my own routine. Clay comes up behind me and whispers as I stand from my last barbell squat in this set to slap my ass. I turn toward him with a pout.

"Baby, as much as I would enjoy a quickie, I'm going out with Penny shortly." I admit.

"I'll make it up to you tonight, you're staying over, right?" He asks like he doesn't already know.

"Apart from when Hadley needed me, I've stayed over only a handful of times." I tease him, "Of course I'll be here."

He smiles sweetly before pressing a chaste kiss on my lips and disappearing into the group training room. The next twenty minutes go by in a blur, sweat drips down my chest and back as I finish my final rep in my final set. I shake my legs and arms out and take a few moments to stretch before I run upstairs to get a quick shower and change. There is a text message waiting for me when I get out of the shower from Penny.

Penny:

> I'm running ten minutes behind, Deke needed to get gas. (eye role emoji)

I chuckle before tapping out my reply.

Kat:

> That actually works out better for me, I just got out of the shower. See you soon, Pen!

Penny:

> See you soon, Love you sis!

With the towel wrapped tightly around my body and chest I rush into the bedroom to grab my clothes. An annoyed groan escapes when I see that he took the shirt. *Damnit, when is he going to just give in and let me have it?* It takes a few minutes to decide on a new shirt, I grab a flowy tank top that accentuates the girls and a pair of jeans that hug my ass beautifully. He's going to lose his mind when he sees me. Especially when he can't touch me any time soon. Serves him right.

With my tits on display, I slide on a pair of converse wedges before I head down to the gym. Clay is still in his class, so I walk over to the door, taking a moment to lean against the doorframe like they do in the romance novels and wait until he looks at me. As soon as his eyes land on me they go wide, I smirk and wink at him before wiggling my fingers to say goodbye. I add a little pep to my step to make my ass pop just a little bit more as I head toward the door where I see Penny and Deke standing together.

"Hey! Are you driving, Hulk?" I ask Deke as I approach them. He only grunts in response, "Ahh such a smooth talker. How do you survive around this man?" I tease both Deke and Penny.

"He's not that bad," she replies quietly. I arch a brow and loop my arm in hers as I lead her outside.

Penny and I have been sitting at this table for a few hours just chatting about everything and anything. Seriously, today she told me that Auggie accidently called her while he was banging either one or both of his girlfriends.

"I never needed to know what my brother getting off sounds like. Gag me." She shivers dramatically as she recalls the event.

We continue our conversation, changing to the topic of some reality show she started watching. Eventually the topic of her plan to get out comes up again but before we can go any further Deke grunts for the tenth time today. I laugh at his ridiculousness, that is until he motions to his watch. Frustration sneaks through my veins with how short our visits have become.

"Damnit, this is stupid!" I whine. "You really do need to get out of there."

"We're working on it. Let's go before he goes Hulk smash on us." She jokes.

To my surprise Deke actually snorts out a laugh when she says it.

"Holy crap, he does have a personality!" I poke at him.

"Car, now." He growls.

So much for that personality.

Deke drove like a psycho to get me back to Karma and all but pushed me out of his car to speed off with Penny. Annoyed, I head inside and up to the apartment. I pull my phone from my pocket and press Clay's contact; I'm debating what to make for dinner. My stomach twists inside me when it rings twice and goes to voicemail. He rejected my call. I stand still as stone as my mind goes through every scenario. Luckily for my overactive imagination, he sends me a text.

Clay:

> Hey Princess, I'll call you in a bit. I just sat to get my hair cut.

I let out a breath. Why am I the way I am? I snort and type out a response.

Kat:

> Not too short right?

Clay:

> I would never dream of taking your hand grips away, I love you.

My lips twitch into a grin and I send another message to see what he wants for dinner, which I don't get a response to right away. Instead of making a decision, because decisions about food are hard; I take a seat on the large couch and turn on my E-reader with the hope of finishing my book. It's just starting to get steamy when my phone lights up on the table in front of me. With a frustrated groan, I lean forward and grab the device to see a text from Clay saying he's bringing someone home to surprise me. Who the hell could he be bringing home that would be a surprise.

Chapter Thirty-Three

My eyes flick to the mirror Kat keeps on the desk to stay aware of her surroundings, fuck. I've been so busy I haven't gotten my hair cut in a few months. The mop on my head looks like a damn Bearded Collie. There is nothing attractive about this look, how the fuck Kat hasn't taken a pair of sheers to my head in the middle of the night is beyond me.

The schedule for the week is just about done. With a quick glance at the time in the bottom right side of the screen, I see it's only two o'clock.

Maybe I'll get lucky and get in to get my hair cut before she gets back from wherever she is with Penny. I rush through finalizing who is coming in before I save the information and power down the device. Sure, this is part of Kat's job, but she had plans today and I offered to take it off her hands. She'll probably just come in and change it tonight.

Thankfully, I took a shower and dressed in street clothes before I sat down I grab my wallet and phone from the desk as I stand. Business has been so good that we've been able to hire on a few more trainers so we generally get more time together than we used to. Quickies in the office are fun, but if I can spread her out on every surface of my...*our*...apartm ent why the hell wouldn't I want to do that? Yeah, hiring the extra help was a good move. I walk toward the front desk to find Ava hunched over the computer typing a response to a social media post comment it looks like.

"Hey Ava, I'm going to head out and see if I can get in to get my hair cut before Kat gets home." My lips turn up into a smile as I think about what I just said. *Home.*

"Ok, you should check out the new place Capi-something Studio. They opened a few weeks ago. I doubt they'd be booked right now. It's only a few blocks over." She responds without lifting her eyes from the computer screen.

"Thanks Ava. I'll see you in a bit." A soft chuckle escapes me as I walk away. She is so focused on what she's doing I could have said I was going to the moon, and she wouldn't have blinked twice.

Sunlight shines down on me as I walk outside. Even though it's bright, the temperature is cool enough that I can walk. I pull my earbuds from my pocket and place them in my ears before finding the latest episode of Manhattan Murder Podcast, some *"sick fuck"* as Lee and Alan would say recently killed someone in the city just outside of the Neon Rose, a bar close to where my mom and I used to live. At least, until the nightmare that brought us to the Midwest. My feet take me into the direction of the new salon that Ava had mentioned without me even thinking about it. I'm so engrossed in the episode it barely registers when I approach the entrance.

A large storefront with bay windows stands before me, a mixture of black, white and teal paint makes up the exterior color palette. It looks very modern, as I step toward the entrance, I see Leigh Adams exiting. I smile and nod politely even if I'd like to throat punch her, but alas; I am a gentleman. The woman rolls her eyes as soon as she sees me and continues walking. I don't bother to hide my amusement as I walk into the building. The interior is just as modern. Black and white paint make up the walls. Every piece of hardware that I can see including the faucets and even the foot pedals on the chairs are rose gold.

What the hell kind of place did I walk into?

"Hi! Welcome to Capelli Studio, do you have an appointment?" A beautiful woman asks as she walks toward me. Her hair is a light brown with streaks of pink at the ends.

"Hi, sorry no. I just happened to have some free time, and I wanted to get my hair cut before my girlfriend gets home from lunch with her sister." I admit as I take her in. Damn she's stunning, her eyes are as blue as the ocean. Kat would be smitten.

"That shouldn't be a problem. My name is Anya, I can take you back and get you done in a jiff. It doesn't look that bad from what I can see. Unless you're hiding more under that hat than meets the eye." she says softly before she winks at me and turns toward the chairs motioning for me to follow her.

"Thanks! I'm Clay. I appreciate you taking me at the last minute like this." My lips twitch into a smirk as I feel her eyes on me.

Her cute button nose scrunches with amusement when I remove my dark blue baseball cap. My hair fans out in all directions as soon as it's free from confinement. I shake my locks free and drag my hand through the messy mane.

"Alright, maybe not a jiff" she giggles before getting started.

Anya wraps the cool black cape around my shoulders and fastens it around my neck. I stare into the mirror at both of us. I'm not sure what it is about this woman but there is something about her that makes me feel like I know her.

She excuses herself for a moment and when she returns she spends five glorious minutes dragging her long fingers through my hair until we decide the length and style to go for. She steps in front of me to grab her clippers when my phone vibrates in my hand. I pull it from under the cape and look down to see an incoming call from Kat, her beautiful face displays on the screen. I press the ignore button to not be rude to the woman with the sharp object near my head and open our text messages.

I chuckle at her response.

I glance back up at the mirror to see Anya staring back at me like she's seen a ghost.

"Hey, are you ok?" I ask, "I'm sorry about that, my girlfriend called and I figured it would be easier if I texted her instead."

Anya shakes her head and smiles brightly.

"I'm great, I actually recognized your girlfriend, I haven't seen her since college, is all." She smirks as she speaks. "Does she still hate the name Pickle?"

"Oh my god, she threatens us any time we say it." I snort. "One of her best girlfriends, Ryan, calls her Pickle constantly just to get a rise out of her."

She continues working as I speak. Kat hasn't seen anyone since she graduated. This could make tonight even better.

"So you and Kat were good friends?" I ask.

"Yea, she was one of my best friends for a while and then life took us in different directions. I'm glad to hear she's doing well." Anya responds as she compares the length of my hair on either side.

"Why don't you come by for dinner tonight? I can have her grab dinner on her way home," I explain. "I just need to talk to her about something which is actually part of the reason, I wanted to get my hair cut today, I think she'd love to see an old friend!"

"Oh, I don't know, I don't want to intrude." She massages some hair gel into her hands before styling my hair for me.

When I find myself in the mirror again, I hardly recognize myself. Damn, I look good.

"Come on, I won't take no for an answer, she would love it." I insist.

"Um, alright." She says hesitantly with a shy smile.

This is going to be an amazing night.

When Anya finishes my hair, she tells me that she can meet us at my place. After squeezing me in she has one more client and then wants to change before she comes over. She lives in the house that backs up to the salon. I snort to myself at that revelation considering I renovated the second floor of my building to be my apartment. We say our goodbyes and I give her my number in case she can't get past Ava.

Chapter Thirty-Four

My curiosity has been driving me mad since I received Clay's text an hour ago saying he has a surprise guest coming home with him for dinner and he was going to order in pizza. Obviously I squashed that, a mystery guest and pizza, not on my watch. Though it makes me anxious as I wonder who the hell could he be bringing.

If it weren't for grocery delivery services I would be lost. I'm in the middle of my makeup and hair when I get the notification that the groceries have been delivered. My hair is only half done as I rush down the stairs to grab the bags and run back upstairs.

I toss some ground sausage in the pan I set on the stove. Then I grab a spatula, light the burner and chop up the meat before walking away to allow it to cook while I quickly dress. By the time I'm back in the kitchen the sausage is browned enough for the next step of Italian seasonings and blended stewed tomatoes. On a second burner, I place a pot of water and turn it on high then wait for it to boil.

My favorite part is mixing in the parmesan cheese and watching it melt into the meat. In a blender I whip heavy cream until it nearly peaks. I pour the whipped cream into the pan with the rest of the sauce and mix it together. The fragrance that fills the kitchen has my mouth watering. I toss the contents of a box of pasta into the boiling water and stir it a few times before I run back to the bedroom.

I have just enough time to finish my hair before the timer I had set on my smart watch goes off to tell me the pasta is ready. I rush back out to the kitchen, drain the water before mixing the pasta and sauce.

The door opens and Clay walks in with the brightest smile. My mouth dries as I take him in, god he's beautiful. His hair is cropped shorter than it was this morning. Still long enough that I can tangle my fingers through but shorter all the same. He's wearing my favorite band tee. The bastard, it looks better on me. Who am I kidding? He can make anything look good. His thick, muscular thighs fill out his dark wash jeans so beautifully. I'm sure if he turned around his thick bubble butt would look even better.

"Hey, Princess!" He crosses the room in a few confident strides and wraps me in a tight embrace. His lips land on mine in an instant, what starts as a soft warm kiss turns into a passionate exchange. Our tongues tangle in a battle for control. I whimper when he nips my now puffy lower lip as he pulls away, forcing us to separate from the exchange.

"Hey, handsome. You look fantastic" I grin up at him, my hands loop around his neck and gaze into his eyes. "What did I do to deserve this greeting?

"I missed you." Clay's grin has my heart racing in my chest.

"You saw me a few hours ago." I roll my eyes at him.

"Exactly, too long." He winks.

"Where is this mystery guest?" I ask, "I've been wracking my brain trying to figure out who it could be."

"They'll be here in a bit. I wanted to talk to you first." He runs his nose up the column of my throat. I let out a soft moan at the delectable contact

"Babe, that's not going to lead to talking and you know that." Chills run through my body as his warm breath skates over my skin.

His husky chuckle has heat searing through me straight to my core. "I wanted to warm you up before I asked my question."

I arch a brow at him, waiting for whatever he's trying to put out there.

"Move in with me," his eyes are hooded with desire.

"Wait, really?" I ask, confused. We've been together for a year but for some reason his words don't make sense.

"You're here more than your own place. Let's make this our home." He smirks something devilish. "I'll officially hand over the shirt when you're moved in."

A wicked giggle passes through my lips. "I would have said yes without the shirt but now that you've put it out there. You can't take it back."

His lips are back on mine, he lifts me with his hands cupping my ass as he presses me hard against him. The hard bulge in his pants is at my center, I moan into his mouth when the intoxicating friction hits my clit. We're both laughing and panting into our kiss as he spins us around when a throat clears. He places me back on my feet and I turn around to see the last person I ever wanted to see.

No. No. No. This can't be happening.

"Hey Anya!" Clay greets her as his arms wrap around my middle, holding onto me from behind.

"Hi, Pickle." She smiles sweetly at the two of us like she didn't just come in and break my heart all over again.

I gasp, her name feels strange on my tongue, like a foreign word long forgotten. My stomach lurches in my belly as I whisper it like the venom it tastes like, "Bunny."

Acknowledgements

My family, your support during this journey has been incredible.

Lori – Happy Birthday, but I'm still not paying for your therapy when you get to the cliffy. Thank you for your love of Pickle, I hope you love her story.

Tiesha – My PA. Lady, I don't know what I would do if you hadn't come into my life. Thank you for all of your hard work and helping me organize my chaos.

My alpha team, you are the MVP and I can't imagine this journey without you.

Sara - My boo. I'll forever be thankful that you slid into my DM's. You are phenomenal, and I love you!

K.D. - My ride or die, I love you and I'm so freaking proud of you!

QS – you ladies keep me sane and I love you.

To the FBI Agent, I hope this one kept you on your toes more than the last one.

Lastly, but most definitely not least, to every single one of you who has reached this page. There will never be enough words for me to express my love for you adequately. Thank you for reading this book. I cannot wait to share additional stories with you!

About the Author

I'm an introvert. Well, until you get to know me. Then I won't shut up. I'm married to my favorite PITA; he's the doctor to my Clara.

(IYKYK). We have a little boy who is growing way too fast and is already way too smart for my own sanity. I've had an unhealthy obsession with *Gilmore Girls* and *Buffy the Vampire Slayer* for years. You'll see the references throughout my writing. I've loved reading for as long as I can remember, but physical books with traditional novel paper give me the ick! So, you'll find me reading on my Kindle or listening to audiobooks on the regular.

Be sure to stalk me on all of my socials here

Also by

Firework - Prequel MM (Joel and Lance's story) coming soon
Endgame
The Unexpected Series
The Unexpected Match Hadley & Connor's Story
The Unexpected FirstRyan and Greyson's Story
The Unexpected Reunion -
The Unexpected Third – MFF – Coming soon
The Unexpected Second Chance - Coming soon

https://mybook.to/ecBnsvTStand Alone - Dark Romance
KILLER IN OUR POCKET - MFF
Stand Alone – Small Town Romance
Pumpkin Spice and Mr. Right